Ch

Confrontation

September 1933 Halifax Yorkshire

When the Norton motorbike skidded to a halt on the wet cobbles, Emily, an attractive brunette, sat glued to her seat behind the driver and glared at the detached millstone house outside which they were parked. She felt fearful, dreading the consequences of confronting her father with a decision she knew he would never approve. '

Are you absolutely sure we need to do this?' She spat out the words slowly in the driver's ear. 'I've lived in that house all my life, yet I'm no longer sure it is still my family. We used to be happy together but over the last few months father has been quite impossible.'

Ever since her teenage years, she had resented the tight control which her parents tried to exercise over her, stifling her along with her spoiled younger sister, Mary. Both had been forbidden to have any boyfriends whose suitability had not been vetted by her father and Emily was determined to wait no longer before escaping from such shackles. She loved Walter dearly – the way he looked at her and treated her as if no other woman existed; his wicked sense of humour, and his intelligence and ambition.

'You know what we agreed', Walter told her as he climbed off his bike. 'Come on, let's get it over with; no point in sitting out here in a thunderstorm.'

They gave one another a big hug, then taking a deep breath to calm her nerves and wiping the raindrops off her face with the back of her hand, Emily reached out and gripped Walter's hand; he squeezed her hand firmly in response. They stood together in silence for a few moments, struggling to pluck up their courage, neither of them quite ready to enter the house.

The weather ended their hesitation with a flash of sheet lightening followed by an ear-shattering clap of thunder. Under dark skies and increasingly heavy rain, Emily glanced at the earnest young man standing beside her, scrabbled in her handbag for the front door key and quickly ushered him into her childhood home.

Still holding hands, they stood dripping on the tiled floor and Emily, biting her lip, stared at the closed lounge door. She could hear the familiar mumble of her father's voice reading aloud from the Bible. Behind that door, she knew he would be sitting bolt upright in his chair still wearing his best black suit kept for use when he delivered sermons as a lay preacher at the local church. The words of the Bible penetrated through the door and caused her to hesitate.

She could picture her mother and young sister, sitting quietly on the dark brown leather settee, hands folded on their laps, waiting with quiet patience for him to finish. A year ago, she would have been sitting there with them.

She felt her hand getting clammy in Walter's grip and, when she glanced at him, noticed that he too looked paler than usual. It gave her some comfort to know that he felt just as nervous as she did. She gave his hand one last squeeze before dropping it, turning the door handle of the lounge with trembling fingers and pushing the door wide open.

Blushing with embarrassment, she blurted out: 'This is Walter Lingard, my fiancé. We are getting married on my twenty first birthday.' That bore little relation to the script which the young couple had spent all day rehearsing, but the pressure of the moment became too great for her to exercise self-control.

Her father put down his Bible and glared at them. 'How dare you burst into the room and interrupt me when I'm reading from the Bible. Now, young lady, would you repeat slowly what you just said?'

Walter tried to intervene, 'Please Sir . . .' he began, but a withering glare from the father abruptly silenced him: 'You, young man, get out of my house NOW.'

Emily knew her father well enough to know he would never change his mind and pleaded with Walter: 'Please go before he throws you out. Your presence only makes matters worse; I love you, you know that,' she sobbed, trying unsuccessfully to hold back her tears. She took his arm and led him quickly to the front door.

As he stepped out onto the drive into the thunderstorm still raging all around, he tenderly cupped her face in his hands, and gave her a quick kiss on the lips. 'Please call me as soon as you can. I need to know that you are safe.'

Emily clasped her arms around the love of her life and kissed him hard on the lips. Then, closing the front door firmly behind her, she wiped her tears away, took a deep breath, tossed her head defiantly, straightened her red polka dot dress and walked back into the lounge with a heavy heart to face her father.

'If you marry that man, you leave this house for good – never to return. NEVER. Do you understand me?' he boomed.

Emily looked at his reddish purple face and knew that he meant every word. How often had she hear him say 'Honour your father and your mother'?

'Look at me when I'm speaking to you. Are you going to obey me?' His words seemed to weave themselves with a slow hiss around his cane as he picked it up from its resting place against the highly polished mahogany sideboard. Emily had rarely seen her father quite so angry; he lost his temper on occasion but usually kept his self-control. Now he seemed beside himself; she could smell the whisky on his breath.

Is the cane merely a threat or does he really intend to use it on me, she thought, remembering all too vividly that as a child he used to bend her over the back of the settee and smack her bottom until she cried. People used to say: 'Spare the rod; spoil the child'. But now I'm a fully grown woman; he won't dare, will he?

Pleading for support, she glanced at her mother, an overweight matronly lady in her fifties who had been subjected to the control of her husband all her married life, sitting wringing her hands together on the couch beside Mary. Emily realised what kept her mother frozen in her seat and vowed that she would never allow herself to become so submissive.

Her mother whispered to her in a low voice, 'Take care not to make your father angry or you'll be in real trouble and I won't be able to stop him. You really shouldn't disturb our Sunday evenings like that; you should be ashamed of yourself.'

Mary, who had remained completely silent throughout the angry exchanges, now suddenly let out a sob which she tried unsuccessfully to stifle. Fearing her husband's rage would be turned on her younger daughter, the mother instantly grabbed the tearful girl and ordered her to bed even though the grandfather clock in the hall had not yet struck nine o'clock. Mary stumbled out of the room, sobbing freely as she climbed the stairs to her bedroom.

Now just the three of them remained in the room. Emily took a moment to survey the scene – her mother on the couch, eyes downcast, shoulders slumped; and her father pacing up and down the dark green carpet square tapping the cane against the palm of his left hand.

How dare he bully her like that and her mother should surely at least make some attempt to stop him. She grimaced at the smell of furniture polish; the faded yellowy brown wallpaper which passed itself off as gold but above all at the brown leather settee where her father used to beat her as a child.

She felt herself begin to tremble, but from anger not fear. At twenty years old she felt to be emancipated and free, not a child to be dictated to by a father she no longer respected. Who did he think he was? Charlie Chaplin. Did he seriously expect her to run upstairs in floods of tears and bend to his will?

Surely, now he must see her as a mature adult and not as just a child whom he could punish with impunity. She looked her father full in the face and, as she glared at him with the full power of her rage, noticed his eyes flicker momentarily.

'Go to your room and stay there until you come to your senses,' he finally roared, slapping the cane against his leg.

Emily turned on her heel and marched smartly out of the room, head held high, and up the stairs to her bedroom next to Mary's room, slamming the door in a vain attempt to shut out the sound of her father ranting about herself and Walter.

Even so his voice penetrated into her eyrie: 'We can't let her marry that street urchin. He has no money, no prospects and spends his time roaring about the place on that motorbike, disturbing all our neighbours. He's the boy I told you about who used to shoot at me with a pea shooter when I delivered groceries to the Co-op in Hebden Bridge and his father is a trade union leader always getting himself into the newspapers.'

Her father felt so strongly about Walter that he might well try to prevent her marriage; at any moment he might burst into her bedroom cane in hand. What would she do if he did?

She flung herself back onto the soft pillows of her bed and stared at the ceiling, reflecting bitterly on the contrast between the way Walter's parents welcomed the news of her engagement and her own parents' reaction to it. 'His father after all is a local celebrity in his own right,' she muttered to herself.

She remembered how proud Walter had been when he told her: 'Apart from my dad's union activities, he puts himself about in the local community, conducting the male voice choir, singing solos in various Methodist chapels and organising celebrities like Gracie Fields to come to local concerts. He is himself a well-known tenor soloist who has won many competitions - even being accorded the honour of singing solo before the King at the Royal Albert Hall. London amazes him, as he says, how does such a city survive with so few mills and so little industry?'

***

Emily's mood changed as she recalled the moment when Walter had proposed to her. It happened one glorious summer day in early June. The weather could not have been more perfect;

windless, warm and a cloudless sky, the blue veiled with a light haze, as it sometimes is in early summer. Even the unforgiving granite rocks scattered around seemed somehow to mellow into the landscape.

Her eyes had filled with tears as she sat in their special place near Hardcastle Crags and watched Walter kneel before her, his voice trembling as he said the words she had been longing to hear for weeks: 'Will you marry me?' Without hesitation, she had responded with an emotional, 'yes!' and thrown her arms around him before smothering him with kisses.

She had danced all the way back to the motorbike holding his hand and humming quietly to herself: 'Sally, Sally in Our Alley'. She pushed all thoughts of her parents' likely disapproval out of her mind, nothing would stop her from getting married to the love of her life.

The very day that Walter proposed to her, they had stopped by his family's house in Hebden Bridge, a small mill town thriving with clothing factories and a dye works which occasionally dyed the river red or blue, to break the good news. His parents' reaction could not have been warmer; they even promised to help make the arrangements for the wedding to take place in their local church.

Emily liked Walter's house – not as grand as her own, but it always seemed friendly and bustling. She liked the informality of friends or relatives entering through the unlocked back door leading into the kitchen. Whenever she visited, the constant flow of friends and neighbours calling in unannounced for a cup of tea and a chat always cheered her.

Walter's father, James, had explained to her: 'All the mill towns enjoy a wakes (holiday) week – always the same week but different weeks for different towns so that resorts like Blackpool can cope with the influx. I always take all our family to St Anne's-on-sea year after year, except for my daughter, Annie, who regularly goes to Switzerland with a party of friends. We go next month; would you like to come with us?' She had politely declined but would always cherish the invitation.

***

The sound of heavy footsteps on the stairs shattered her daydreaming. Father! She sat bolt upright on her bed and clasped her hands together – dreading what might happen next. Her father flung open the bedroom door and stood over her, with the cane held tightly in his right hand.

'Have you come to your senses yet, daughter?' he growled in a calm menacing voice, tapping the cane in his hand against his leg. For a moment, the pink flowers on the wall behind him blurred into a pink fog.

'Please,' she gasped in alarm. 'I want to respect you, I am your daughter. I need time to sort myself out.'

He snorted. 'Take care you do as I say or you'll regret it. There will be no wedding to that young man you brought home. I've discussed the matter with your mother and we do know one or two young men who would make a suitable husband. I'll talk to their parents and arrange for them to come to dinner and meet you.'

'Who are they?' gasped Emily in alarm.

'You'll find out in good time when I'm ready,' her father barked, with which he left slamming the door behind him.

Emily sat back on her bed and allowed herself a little smile, relieved that no violence had been inflicted on her person. 'We will see about that,' she thought. 'No matter what my parents do, I'm going to marry Walter on my twenty-first birthday and nothing they do will stop me. By law, I'll then be free to marry whomsoever I please without their consent.'

She banged her fists against the pillow and a tear rolled down her cheek; it should never have come to this. 'Why can't my father see Walter's qualities and his ambitions to succeed and see the world? My clever Jimmy has been awarded a Fulbright scholarship to Harvard University in America and wants to take me with him.'

She knew that her father could not stand Walter's father who seemed to court publicity wherever he went but Walter bore little resemblance to his father in that respect; her fiancé shunned publicity, vowing to lead a sober respectable life.

***

Next morning, Emily woke up with an even stronger determination to disobey her parents' wishes. Not wanting to risk further confrontation, she remained in her bedroom sanctuary until her father left the house, then dressed hurriedly in her work clothes of white blouse and long grey skirt and ran downstairs. Without stopping for breakfast, she uttered a curt: 'See you this evening' to her mother and rushed out of the house.

Desperate to get to work, she wanted to reassure Walter and let him know that nothing had changed despite her parents' disapproval, that their plans were still in place, to give him her very own go ahead. Her father's obstinacy and mother's lack of support would not make her change her mind – the decision she had made was final. She ended the call with a nervous giggle and whispered 'I love you so much' then sat back in her chair and sighed with happy relief.

Emily hugged her secret to herself, determined not to let any of her friends on the switchboard in on her plans. If their gossip filtered through to her father, it could be disastrous. Despite her nervous excitement, she managed to make it through the rest of the working day, grateful to focus her mind on something else for a time.

When she arrived home from work that evening, Emily could hear her father and mother talking quietly in the kitchen. She took off her coat, straightened her shoulders and with her head held high walked steadily into the room: 'Please may I eat supper on a tray in my room, I need to be alone.'

Emily knew what that would mean in a family which always ate their dinner together but simply could not face being with her parents after the previous night's altercation. Her father glared at her, but agreed to her request sending her off with just bread and jam and a cup of tea. Emily gave him a curt nod and took a tray up to her room, relieved that there would be no more rows that night.

This strict regime continued for the next two days but Emily needed life in the family home to go as smoothly as possible in order to allay her parents' suspicions that she might still be intending to marry Walter. That would be disastrous; so on the Wednesday she decided to be on her very best behaviour and resume dining with her parents. It would all be worthwhile if she succeeded in eloping and marrying her Jimmy.

After dinner, she found herself alone with her father for the first time that week. She had been careful to avoid any confrontation between them but now he looked serious. 'Well my girl, I've done my best and I have found you a suitable husband.' Emily simply nodded and wished her father goodnight; it really didn't matter who he had in mind or did it?

***

Chapter 2

Trouble

As her twenty first birthday came closer, Emily began to realise just how easily her father could sabotage her plans if he discovered them. He would not be able to prevent her marrying Walter but they needed to catch their steamer to America after the ceremony and even two hours delay could make them miss it. She knew that her plans must be kept secret to have any chance of success and resolved to cooperate with her parents however outrageous their demands.

So on the Wednesday three days before her wedding, she stood with her head bowed behind a dining room chair whilst her father said his usual lengthy grace. After it, he paused and added in a superior tone of voice: 'Before we sit down, I have an important announcement to make'. Emily looked up discomforted to find him staring steadily at her, wearing a tight smile; her stomach knotted in fear.

'On Friday, we're having the Halifax Building Society manager, John Boothroyd, and his wife, Maud, over to dinner. They are bringing Lionel, their eldest son, to meet you. Lionel is just the sort of young man you should be mixing with.'

Emily tried to control the hot flush of anger that swept through her as she glared at the short plump man with his ridiculous ginger toothbrush moustache. At twenty years old she felt to be emancipated and free like her heroine, the suffragette

Mary Ann Rawle, not a child to be dictated to by a father whom she no longer respected. Drawing herself up to her full five feet eight inches tall, she looked her father full in the face.

How could he do this? Did he really think that her head would be turned by a man just because he came from a 'respectable' family? She looked down at one of her favourite meals - guinea fowl, spinach and new potatoes - and felt sick; her father's announcement had killed her appetite. She took a deep breath and turned her gaze to her mother. 'May I please be excused?' she pleaded.

Her mother shook her head slowly, her eyes blazing with annoyance at her daughter's impudence. 'No you may not my girl,' her father roared. 'And what's more, you will be on your best behaviour on Friday night. There will be hell to pay if you embarrass yourself or your family.'

Nobody said a word for several minutes after that; Emily spent the rest of the meal with her head bowed, eating as little of her dinner as she considered necessary to placate her parents. She had grown up submitting to their will but this time a thought could not leave her head: 'I must get away from here and from my parents, these people are stifling me.'

***

That evening, Emily looked around her expensively decorated bedroom, adorned with pink floral wall-paper, and knew that her father looked upon his house as a status symbol. Well, there are far more important things in life than living in a big house, she told herself.

'My boyfriend, Walter, is an educated man whose ambitions will take him far away from Halifax; he went to the grammar school, graduated from university with a first class degree, holds a highly respectable job as a bank clerk at Lloyds Bank and I love him. Surely that's enough for any parent? It isn't Walter's fault that he comes from a working class background with a trade union leader as his father.'

The prospect of elopement added a thrill to what in any event promised to be the most exciting day in her life. But it wasn't just the wedding she looked forward to; over the last few weeks she and her husband to be had been secretly storing clothes in two steel cabin trunks tucked away in his father's house.

Immediately after the wedding, the newlyweds planned to travel to Liverpool and catch a Cunard liner to take up Walter's Fulbright scholarship. She confided to her favourite doll: 'I'm going to escape from Halifax and my domineering father. I really am and perhaps I will never come back. Just fancy, America!'

Emily knew little about what to expect in America. She had read a number of cowboy stories and watched films about the Keystone Cops and the exploits of Charlie Chaplin. She laughed at Abbot and Costello but also remembered having heard from her father about the terrible Stock Exchange crash on Wall Street in 1929. What would life in the United States really be like?

She realised that her parents would never approve of her marrying into a lower class than themselves. They were class conscious and in their eyes, such a marriage would impact on their own social standing; they expected her to marry a man of an equal if not better class. The string of 'suitable' young men they kept encouraging her to meet made this obvious but her heart led her down a different path.

She loved Walter dearly; life with him would be an adventure and she craved excitement. And yet, throughout her courtship she still tried hard to respect her mother's guidance. There were plenty of soft passionate kisses and breathless cuddles, but she fought her desires and honoured the dictum drummed into her by her parents as soon as she learned about the birds and the bees – no sex before marriage.

Emily clenched her fists in frustration, fed up with being a good girl. Well – no more. She needed to be free to live her own life with Walter and planned to marry him on her birthday, the very next Saturday. She had heard gossip of girls being forced to bow to their parents' wishes. Her own father felt so strongly about Walter that he might well try to prevent her marrying him.

She reflected on just what she wanted out of life; what really mattered to her? First and of paramount importance, she must marry Walter; her whole future depended on that. Secondly, she needed to escape from her parents for good and start a family of her own free from their interference.

Equally important, she saw marriage as a partnership of equals, not a dictatorship like her parents' marriage, and felt confident that Walter shared this view even if most of the local boys did not. Once they were married, she would be well on the way to achieving these objectives provided she could persuade her new husband to treat her as an equal, a chance she needed to take.

Her mood lightened as she remembered how their romance began. Before leaving school, she really knew nothing of the real world; her father, who knew the local manager, found her a job with the Halifax Building Society, not even allowing her to choose her own career.

She hated the routine office job her father expected her to do but, when the opportunity arose, opted for a vacancy on the telephone switchboard which most people regarded as having the same prestige as the receptionists. Every day she spoke to scores of customers, a tremendous variety of characters – some of whom even attempted to flirt with her.

The other telephonists, far more street-wise, took her into their group. They called her 'Bubbles', a nickname reflecting her cheerful smiles and optimistic approach to life which made her popular. So attractive a girl seemed obviously in need of their guidance about how to handle boyfriends.

One of them, with a brother at the local grammar school, had procured her an invitation to a Christmas dance which it had organised for recent school leavers. Her friends soon paired off with other local boys, leaving Emily alone knowing none of the men there and feeling out of her depth as she sat tapping her feet to the ragtime jazz.

Then out of the swirling couples emerged one of the school's old boys about her own age, perhaps a couple of inches taller and a stone or so heavier, who looked to be coming straight towards her. She could feel her heart beating a little bit faster as he approached. He smelt of carbolic soap and his long dark hair fell over his face, not parted in the middle and plastered down with greasy smelly hair cream like so many of the others.

He gave her a wide smile and holding out his hand asked her to dance. Laughing, she took his hand, which felt cool to her touch, and walked with him towards the balloon-decked section of the school gymnasium set aside for dancing.

'I'm Walter,' he announced 'Do you dance the Charleston?' As she shook her head sorrowfully and tried to say she would like to try, he interrupted her with, 'I know who you are. You're Bubbles!'

Emily laughed, feeling her face grow warm. 'Bubbles is a childish name,' she blushed. 'Why not call me Betty? It's not my real name but I like it and it can be our secret.'

Walter smiled. 'Well, if you're going to be Betty, then I'll be Jimmy!' he joked.

They spent the rest of the evening dancing boogie-woogie and swing and chatting to each other about their past lives and families and hopes for the future. When it all came to an end, Walter gently stroked her arm and for the first time that night suddenly looked a bit nervous. Emily smiled at him in encouragement; finally, Jimmy blurted out: 'I have a motorbike. Would you like to go for a run up to the moors next Saturday? I can show you some truly magnificent views of range upon range of hills stretching out to the horizon.'

Emily hesitated; she wanted to see Walter again but going on a motorcycle with a boy she had just met seemed unwise? Her parents would be horrified! Emily looked into his twinkling blue eyes which, as far as she could see, held nothing but admiration for her and happily accepted.

She would never forget the experience, the exuberance of being on the back of such a powerful machine with the wind in her hair - no one wore crash helmets in those days. Then kissing her first real boyfriend, his happy fascinating eyes and the way he stroked her arm and treated her like a princess. She had never known such polite deference and tenderness.

After that, the two of them spoke every day on the telephone, using their pet names for each other, Jimmy and Betty, in the hope that this would fool any girl on the switchboard who happened to be listening to their conversation.

Most weekends, Emily would jump on the back of Walter's motorbike and they would speed off to Hardcastle Crags - a well-known beauty spot near Hebden Bridge with a startling granite outcrop carved out by the fast flowing river which had washed away the surrounding sandstone to create a gorge. These outings took priority over all other invitations to excursions or parties which either of them received; a mystery which caused some suspicion and gossip amongst the other switchboard girls.

There the loving couple had spent hours sitting on a fallen tree trunk, talking, kissing and laughing; gradually becoming more passionate in their embraces as the weeks went by, but he always respected her decision on when to stop.

She chuckled at the memory of whispering in her lover's ear on one occasion when she felt her body becoming too aroused: 'Ooh! Did you see the Kingfisher flash passed? Isn't its royal blue plumage truly magnificent?' When the ruse worked and he broke away in his excitement to see the bird, she added: 'I do like lying on my back in the sun watching the rabbits frolicking about, listening to the bird song, and smelling the fragrance of the wild flowers and the heather. Can we make this our special place?'

On one occasion, Walter drew a small pencil portrait of his princess. 'Would you like this picture? I'm rather proud of the way it's turned out,' he offered hesitantly. She blushed: 'Thanks. Do I really look like that? I'll always treasure it and carry it around in my handbag.'

***

For Emily, Friday's dinner with her boss and his family seemed to arrive all too soon. Working away at the Building Society switchboard, she felt sad at the thought of the ordeal about to be inflicted on her. However, the dinner gave her an excuse to visit the hairdresser and indulge in a lavish hair style for her wedding.

Normally, without her parents' knowledge, she would go for a quick drink with her colleagues after work on a Friday, but not today. She chose her words carefully before cheerily announcing to them, 'I can't come out with you all tonight as I have to help my mother with a dinner party. Lionel is coming over with his parents.'

The switchboard girls regularly gossiped about this bachelor in his thirties who had a reputation for not being able to keep his hands to himself. Several of them claimed to have slept with him but it would be no use telling her parents that, they simply would not believe it - at least there could be no danger of her falling for the brute.

After work, she walked home with her switchboard friend, Elsie, who lived in the next street. Usually full of chat and gossip, the girl fell strangely silent, stopped in the middle of the cobbled street and knitted her fingers together: 'I swore never to tell anyone and if I do tell you, you must promise to keep my secret,' she whispered. Emily put one hand on her friend's arm to comfort her and nodded.

'Two months ago, Lionel invited me to a party at his house and I got a little drunk. He took me into his father's study, shut the door and told me he'd always wanted to have sex in that room.'

Emily looked at her friend's distraught expression and was appalled; that Lionel clearly must be a monster. She squeezed Elsie's arm gently encouraging her to continue, although dreading to hear what might have happened next.

Elsie, took a deep breath and continued shakily, 'I told him I wouldn't do any such thing with him, but then he lost his temper. He grabbed me by the hair, bent me over the back of a chair and spanked me hard. I suppose I'm lucky not to have been raped.'

Emily threw her arms around her good friend and hugged her close. When the two women broke apart, she thanked Elsie for warning her about Lionel.

'Just make sure you're not alone with him,' Elsie sobbed, her eyes filling with tears.

Emily promised to be careful, said goodbye to her friend and walked home struck by a heavy sadness. She kept repeating to herself: 'Why oh why father are you even considering such a horrible man as a suitable husband for me?' She tried to imagine what it would be like to be married to a perverted philanderer and the thought made her feel ill.

That evening, Emily wore her second best dress, a dark green taffeta. Her mother expressed pleasant surprise at the choice and complemented her on the new hair style, clearly relieved that her daughter seemed finally to be complying with her parents' wishes.

Lionel duly arrived with his parents promptly at a quarter to seven. Despite everything she had heard about him, part of her could see why the girls at work gossiped about such an impressive handsome-looking man and why her father considered him to be such a prize. He held himself well, making the most of his six-foot frame, and wore a smart brown double-breasted suit and waistcoat.

Lionel smiled at her and held out his hand. Her heart gave a momentary flutter; could this superb Adonis really be interested in her? But when she took the hand, any thoughts of admiration evaporated at the feel of his limp, clammy handshake and the smell of the hair cream which smothered the thick blond hair parted down the middle of his head.

Her father took the visitors' coats and ushered Lionel's parents into the lounge for some drinks before dinner, remarking: 'We'll leave the youngsters to introduce themselves.'

As soon as the lounge door closed, Lionel quietly announced: 'I know all about your boyfriend who goes tearing round the neighbourhood on his motorbike. You're Bubbles, one of the switchboard girls in my father's office. Most of your colleagues like a bit of fun. I expect you do as well?'

Emily gave an involuntary shudder of distaste as she shook her head. In spite of his masculine frame, he spoke in a high-pitched voice which added to the list of disagreeable things about him. She quickly looked away and tried her best to ignore him. A bit of fun? With him? – Ugh, the very last thing she wanted.

But instead of taking the hint, Lionel moved closer: 'I should like to give you a hug. May I? I must say you are much more attractive than most of your colleagues.'

Without waiting for Emily to respond, he put his hands on her shoulders, gently pulled the surprised girl towards him and gave her a kiss on the cheek. The kiss became a hug, and Emily wasn't quite sure what to do. A kiss on the cheek seemed fairly harmless, didn't it?

She did not resist but then his right hand began slowly to move down her back inch by inch. Before she could break away from him, he whispered in her ear, 'nice breasts,' and simultaneously squeezed her bottom. Furious, she pushed him away, and took a step backwards intending to deliver a hard slap across his smirking face.

He raised an arm to block the blow, muttering sulkily, 'You can't hit me – you're only a girl,' and then strode over to the lounge door and turned the knob with unnecessary force. He shut the door before she could follow him into the room and she found herself standing alone in the cold hallway in her second-best dress wondering what to do next.

She eyed the front door, imagining walking straight out into the cold night air, never to return. Sighing, she turned away to face the lounge; running away would probably result in the police being called and hunting her down. She must somehow get through the evening and ignore that oily fool if he tried anything again. Another time he might even go too far in front of her father.

As she turned to enter the room, the door opened and the party moved into the dining room. Although she didn't want to be anywhere near Lionel, she took the chair at the table assigned to her by her father between Lionel and himself.

To distract herself, she raised her bowed head a little to look around the dining room with its dark red patterned wallpaper and floral curtains. She always considered it to be the pleasantest room in the house. It made her think about happier times - past birthdays and Christmases. Surreptitiously, she slipped her hand under the white table cloth and felt comforted by the cool smoothness of the highly polished mahogany table.

As soon as her father finished saying grace, Lionel tucked into the food in front of him and wolfed it down oblivious to the fact that all the others were eating much more slowly. Emily ignored his bad manners as best she could and savoured every bite of the superb roast beef and Yorkshire pudding. She reflected that the cook, an employee of her father, brought in to prepare and serve the meal never pretended to be a chef.

As she tackled the last of her boiled cabbage, Lionel leaned over and whispered: 'You really do appeal to me as a most gorgeous girl. You and I could have lots of fun together upstairs.' Staying true to her decision to ignore him at all cost, she continued eating as if he hadn't spoken.

Lionel changed tack and began to give a long-winded, pompous account of his sporting prowess, which Emily felt sure must be exaggerated. He finished one story with '. . . and then in the cricket match against Keighley, I made a terrific catch at head height right on the boundary. It would have been a six otherwise.'

He paused, and looked directly at Emily, clearly waiting for a response. Although Emily never liked cricket, she felt obliged to say something, especially as everyone around the table seemed to be looking at her.

'Isn't that what boundary fielders are supposed to do?' she enquired as innocently as she could. To her surprise, everyone laughed at this - everyone apart from Lionel who threw her a dark look and stared at his empty plate. Good, Emily thought, far better if he decided that she would not be the girl for him after all.

When the plates were cleared away, Emily rose to help her mother supervise the preparation of the final course, relieved to have a break from sitting next to Lionel. On returning to the dining room, she discovered that his chair seemed to have been moved closer to hers, his right thigh almost touching her left. She gritted her teeth and vowed not to let her unpleasant neighbour destroy her appetite for her favourite dessert – fruit salad and cream. While she savoured its delicious sweetness, her thoughts turned to just how she should escape from the house when the time came to elope.

A sudden pressure on her left thigh broke her out of her reverie; she looked down and found Lionel's massive hand resting on her knee. She tried to brush it away but he closed his grip more firmly. Emily thought about announcing his appalling conduct to the rest of the table, but worried that nobody would believe her; least of all her father who, judging by his smiles and nods towards Lionel, considered him to be the best young man to have visited the house in years.

Taking a deep breath, Emily decided to continue to ignore the hand but, to her dismay, it started very slowly to edge higher up her thigh. Things were getting out of hand.

'Really,' she exclaimed in a loud voice turning on Lionel. He removed his hand instantly, but his expression remained unruffled.

'I simply wondered if Emily and I could put a record on the gramophone and dance in the lounge rather than stay in here and drink coffee with you,' he explained politely to Emily's father.

She bit her lip when her father approved the suggestion with a delighted, 'of course!' What she wanted seemed to be of no significance; five minutes later loud waltz music filled the house and she found herself in Lionel's arms. He held her much closer than politeness required and his right hand soon began to stray again.

Mindful of her conversation with Elsie, she glanced around for a weapon with which to defend herself if things got out of hand. The poker on the hearth seemed an obvious choice, and she decided to use it if he tried anything further.

Lionel waltzed her towards one side of the room and stared at her father's cane resting on the sideboard. He gave her a smirk, as if he knew exactly what he would like to do if he got his hands on that cane.

The record finished and when he broke away to change it, Lionel reached across from the gramophone and picked up the cane. 'Time to liven you up my girl, we'll play something nice and loud.'

But Emily had remembered all too clearly what happened to poor Elsie and already stood near the door. The time to ignore this fool was over. 'That is quite enough of that!' she exploded. 'Leave me alone you horrible man!'

All of a sudden, a return to the dining room and the safety of her own family appeared to be a safe option; she stormed out of the lounge and returned to the dinner party. Lionel marched in a couple of minutes later with the same smirk on his face. For the rest of the evening, she behaved as if he was not there.

The guests left close to midnight and Emily found herself alone with her father. 'Well my girl, Lionel will be coming over at around 12 noon tomorrow and he'll take you out for lunch. You could do a lot worse than him; he's got real prospects of a good career at the Building Society.'

Emily simply nodded and wished him goodnight. How sad her father thought that a man so much older than herself and so conceited would make a suitable husband. Well, she had other ideas and the sooner they came to fruition the better, by 12 noon tomorrow she would be far away from Halifax!

***

Chapter 3

Eloping

Emily did not sleep at all that night; she worried about whether her decision to elope had been sensible. What if her father was right and her motor cycle boyfriend proved to be rough with her or unreliable? Did she really know him, after all they had never actually slept together?

As midnight passed she dismissed such heresy and told herself: 'I need to be awake and ready to leave when my Jimmy arrives. If I fail him, I might be forced to marry Lionel – imagine that huge, repulsive man forcing himself upon me!' She shuddered and her thoughts returned to the more urgent preparations for her journey. 'My first priority must be to pack all my essentials into a knapsack.'

That proved more difficult than she expected; it took over an hour agonising over what to take and what to leave, there would be no second chance to recover anything which she forgot. 'Time now to say goodbye to my childhood collection of dolls and family photographs, before consigning them to a cupboard. A shame I shall never see them again but it can't be helped.'

She checked and rechecked a list of what she needed and what must be done. 'Too much clobber, do I really need to take any books? I can always buy another copy of *Alice in Wonderland*. What have I done with my hair brush?'

'Should I leave a note or simply disappear? If I don't, the police will spend hours looking for me; but if I do and the note is found before we're married, the result could be disastrous. Then again, what should I write?' In the end, she decided it would be safer to do nothing.

At four o'clock in the morning, she dressed in her travelling clothes and thought for the hundredth time about how she might leave the house without being heard. 'I must take more care with my make up; my Jimmy needs to see me looking at my best.'

Her original idea of knotting the sheets from her bed together and climbing out of the bedroom window lost its appeal when she opened it and looked out. A full moon in a clear sky promised a fine dry day ahead, but also brightly lit the entire street below. To her horror, she spotted the local policeman patrolling down the road.

'Knotted sheets hanging from a window will attract his attention and he'll raise the alarm. My father knows the Chief Constable and he'll have Jimmy arrested for abducting me if I'm caught with him. It's no good; I'll have to creep out through the front door and pray that nobody hears me.'

She kept looking at her watch but time seemed to stand still. Perhaps Walter would come early? She began to peep out of the window every few minutes, but the empty street only made her start biting her nails and she knew that would spoil them.

At last 4.30 am arrived and when she looked out of the window, there he stood across the street looking up anxiously towards her bedroom; her Jimmy – waiting for her just as he promised. Filled with a new energy, she opened the sash window enough to give him a cheery wave and blow him a kiss. No sign of the policeman. As soon as he saw her, he gave an enormous grin and waved back. A rush of relief swept through her; Walter at last - time to act.

She opened her bedroom door inch by inch and peeped out just as the toilet flushed in the bathroom at the end of the landing. A quick look revealed her parents' bedroom door to be wide open, so she ducked back into her room and closed the door softly, her heart beating fast – shaken at the narrow escape.

Hearing her father return to bed, she grabbed her knapsack and crept out of the bedroom, tip-toeing across the landing and down the stairs. 'I must avoid the seventh step which always creaks. Now, where on earth is the front door key? No, not in its usual place in the drawer of the small table next to the hat stand. But we always keep it there!'

She wasted precious time hunting for the key, before deciding that perhaps her father had removed it deliberately. 'Hell, am I locked into the house? I'm going to have to trade my dignity for freedom and climb through a window - - perhaps the key to the kitchen door is still in the drawer next to the sink.'

Footsteps above caused her to skid to a halt in the hallway; to her dismay they seemed to be moving towards the stairs. She dashed through the partly-open lounge door, hid behind the settee and peeped out, just in time to see her father in his dark blue dressing gown walking by.

Moments seemed like hours as she waited in the dark. 'Did he hear me leave the bedroom despite all the care I took? Is he looking for me?' Then the sound of running water: 'What a relief, he only wants a glass of water,' she sighed.

Emily waited breathlessly until the sound of heavy footsteps going up the stairs told her she could now safely run into the kitchen, and let herself out of the back door. The key lay invitingly on the tiled work top but as she struggled with both hands to undo the stiff top bolt, her knapsack slipped off the table and knocked off a cup which smashed onto the floor.

Did anyone hear? She listened intently, from above came the sound of her father's voice: 'I heard a noise downstairs. You stay here in bed whilst I see if everything is locked up properly.' She gritted her teeth: 'What am I going to do? If I run for it, he'll chase after me or worse call the police and have Walter arrested. --- Don't panic; take the key with you and lock the door from the outside.'

Running through the cool leafy garden around to the side alleyway and through the front gate, she fell into her lover's arms and pulled him out of sight of the house. She took a step back, looked at her Jimmy, smiled and kissed him then kissed him again and again passionately. 'I've escaped! I really have, but father's suspicious, we must get away from here.' He grabbed her hand and together they ran down the street, Emily could almost feel the adrenalin pumping in her veins at the excitement of what they were about to do.

When they turned the corner into the next street, Jimmy explained to her: 'I've brought dad's car; it's over there'. Emily saw a black Austin Cambridge saloon parked on the other side of the road. 'It's less conspicuous and quieter than the motorbike,' he added breathlessly.

As Walter drove back to Hebden Bridge, he explained: 'In the absence of your parents, my Dad will be giving you away at the church. He likes you, but it's me that you are marrying! I don't want any last minute change of mind.' Emily giggled; finally all their carefully made plans were falling into place.

Emily confided about being threatened with the cane. Walter squeezed her hand: 'I'm so sorry. My Dad never used a cane to teach us a lesson, he wore a thick leather belt in addition to his bracers and used that if I disobeyed him as I know to my cost.'

They drove on in silence through Sowerby Bridge then Walter continued: 'Dad's latest activities have made him something of a hero in Hebden Bridge. It's possible the local paper may be at our wedding. He promised the media that if they attended the John Lewis store in Leeds at a certain time, he would provide them with a story. True to his word, he sprang on to a counter and announced: "People of Leeds, this store is selling foreign goods. Buy British. Be patriotic and support your own community."

'The store manager assured everyone: "I would love to buy British but the goods are too expensive."

'Dad insisted on being given the key figures in writing but management in Hebden Bridge claimed they could not match such low prices. He then addressed a mass meeting of the workers: "If you work one day a week at today's wages, your families starve. If you work four days a week at lower wages, you eat with enough over for a pint or two." He won the vote by a huge margin, enabling a new contract to be negotiated with the store and saving the town from a great deal of suffering.'

As they neared Hebden Bridge, the realisation struck Emily that she would shortly be marrying into a family she barely knew. 'Tell me about your mother's background and your sister, Annie, who's going to be my bridesmaid,' she implored.

'Oh, you need not worry about Annie, she's quite harmless and totally supportive of what we're doing. She sings with our local light opera society; it's her hobby and she regularly performs leading roles in Gilbert and Sullivan operettas.

'As for my mother, her parents died some years ago. Her father did once make the headlines in the local paper. Hebden Bridge in those days exploded into drunken violence on Saturday nights. Factory workers were paid on Friday and many watched Halifax Town or Huddersfield play football, then retired to a pub to celebrate victory or drown their sorrows.

'When the pubs closed, fights often broke out. The police only intervened if the violence got out of hand. They deployed a giant of a sergeant, much feared locally, who routinely smashed the drunks into submission with his truncheon.

'Ada's father objected and in the resulting struggle floored the sergeant and confiscated his truncheon. No one dared arrest him and the police were too embarrassed to charge him to the outrage of the press.'

That did not seem at all harmless to Emily; she found herself about to marry into a family of tenor and soprano soloists who regularly performed in public. Would she be able to live up to the high standards which such people expected?

The nearer they came to Hebden Bridge, her doubts about getting married increased. Her parents had questioned Walter's suitability as a match for her, but she had never considered her own suitability for him and fell into a moody silence. As if sensing her uncertainty, Walter gave her hand a reassuring squeeze. Grateful for the touch, she squeezed it back.

When they arrived in Hebden Bridge, she rushed into his arms and gave him a great big hug which took his breath away: 'Being with you is the most important thing in my life; I've never been so sure about anything.' Hand in hand they marched up the steep hill to Walter's home – to the house where he had lived all his life and, like her, would soon be leaving behind.

***

As they approached the small two bedroom terrace house built of millstone grit where James and his family lived, Emily reflected on what she knew about their way of life. It boasted a sizeable kitchen dominated by a large washing machine, topped by a pair of rollers for squeezing water out of the clean clothes. Walter's mother, Ada, spent every Monday toiling at that machine, washing and ironing for the entire family.

Ada might not have known how much her husband earned or what he did with his money but Emily admired her achievement in prevailing upon him to sign the pledge to stop drinking alcohol. This did not prevent him from hiding a bottle of his favourite port in the cellar; the thought of a sip or two assisted in motivating him to fill the coal scuttle in cold weather. Jimmy had explained that the steep concrete cellar steps provided a degree of security from Ada whose bad leg, caused by severe eczema, prevented her from descending them.

The kitchen opened onto a compact living room with its coal fire and Aga stove for cooking; the supply of logs or coal kept the fire hot enough to heat the room. All meals were eaten at the table in this room, starting with breakfast which in James' case consisted of a pint mug of strong coffee, taken early enough for him to arrive at work no later than 8am.

On Sundays, the whole family would attend one of the local Methodist chapels founded by John Wesley, who a century earlier came to preach in the then godless area. After the service, they usually enjoyed roast beef and roast potatoes for lunch; the family ate well.

The house also contained a front room (lounge), normally left unheated and only used to entertain strangers or for singing practice or on rare occasions to listen to a powerful wireless set. This vied with the upright piano topped by a metronome as the focal point for the brown settee and two matching easy chairs. The house always benefitted from electricity and main drainage, unlike some in the vicinity whose occupants were forced to use an outside toilet.

Apart from Ada with her bad leg, the family spent little time at home. Up early, working late, music practice and social engagements filled the day.

When the happy couple arrived, the front door opened and there stood Ada, Emily's mother in law to be, a slim woman with streaks of grey in her hair who smiled kindly at them. She gave the prospective bride a quick hug and said: 'Welcome home! The house is a bit chaotic at the moment with all the preparations for your wedding, but I will run a hot bath for you. May I suggest you go straight to the bathroom whilst we prepare breakfast and please leave the bathwater for Walter when you finish. We're short of hot water.'

Emily undressed quickly and slid into the warm water, resting her head against the edge of the bath. She thought about marriage and what it might mean. Her forehead creased a little as she thought about the wedding night; she couldn't help but feel a bit nervous – it would be her first time after all.

A moment of panic flashed through her mind: 'What if Walter is rough with me? He might be a brute like Lionel. What if he forces himself on me before I'm ready; marriage gives irrevocable consent to sex,' she thought. Suddenly, she didn't want to get out of the bath and face the rest of the day.

A light tap on the door made her sit up; Walter. 'Is everything alright, Emily?' he sounded concerned. 'I forgot to suggest that you use my dressing gown hanging on the back of the door. Breakfast is ready and my sister has your clothes in her room.'

Her heart softened; bless him, he seems so anxious. The sound of his voice comforted her; she smiled to herself: 'He thinks of everything.' Her heart lifted – she couldn't wait to get married.

Besides, she'd better hurry because any minute now her parents would discover her empty bedroom and possibly call the police.

She quickly dried herself, slipped on Walter's dressing gown and opened the door just as her future father in law emerged from his bedroom. 'If I'm to give you away, I need to be sure that you really do want to marry my son,' he told her.

She blushed, not least because she had nothing on underneath the dressing gown, and assured him: 'I do love Walter dearly, I really do and always will'. He misinterpreted her discomfort and gave her a quick hug. The gown fell open revealing all! She felt mortified, but he pretended not to see and went downstairs.

***

Annie and the girl who did make-up for the Light Opera Society took Emily into the back bedroom and touched up her nails, make-up and hair before she stepped into the wedding dress and tried on the veil. She had deliberately chosen a strapless short white dress which showed off her figure without trailing on the ground.

When they finished, both agreed she looked gorgeous and Emily beamed at their compliments; but as wedding tradition dictated, they would not allow her to go downstairs until Walter had left the house. Meanwhile the best man, a lifelong friend of Walter, arrived with flowers for all the family and took charge of the bridegroom, hustling him off to help decorate the church in time for the 8.30 am service.

The wedding followed tradition as closely as possible, except that none of the bride's family and friends were present. A crowd of well-wishers, supporters of James and Annie, more than made up for their absence.

Walter's father gave her away, whispering words of encouragement and compliments as they walked down the aisle. She felt grateful for his support and appreciated his efforts to welcome her into his family. By the time she finally reached Walter in his smart Sunday best dark grey suit, she could not stop smiling, thrilled to see the look of admiration in his eyes.

Although the congregation had no choir to lead it, both the groom's father and sister sang the hymns with great gusto. When the couple made their vows, Emily dutifully promised to obey her husband and smiled to see his eyes shine with pride. Such a promise contradicted her beliefs about marriage being a partnership of equals, but she knew all brides were expected to make it. She just wanted the wedding to be over and made the vow in order to get married.

As the service progressed and nine o'clock approached, Emily grew more and more worried that one of the strangers at the back of the church might object to the wedding. Only when they were declared man and wife did she relax. Although she felt elated throughout, it came as a relief when the ceremony ended without interruption.

It had been a lovely ceremony but there would be no time for celebrations; the newlyweds and their close relatives and friends rushed to the station. They needed to catch the train to Manchester from where they would take the boat train to Liverpool. Their train came chugging into view, hissing and spitting steam all over everybody. James had reserved two second class compartments for close friends and they spilled into them as soon as the guard marched down the platform and unlocked the doors.

During the entire half hour journey to Manchester, Emily clutched Walter's hand tightly. She kept worrying: 'What have I done? I've given myself to Jimmy and even promised to obey him. He looks so pleased with himself. I'm safe enough on the train and where there are people about but how will he behave when we are alone? Will he treat me as a slave - his father is very dominating?'

She squeezed her new husband's hand and when he responded by doing the same smiled in relief and pushed her anxieties aside. Everything had happened so rapidly that she could hardly take it all in, but they were finally married and she wore a ring on her finger and possessed a wedding certificate to prove it.

***

Chapter 4

The Honeymoon

The wedding party arrived at the check-in hall for the Cunard liner to find it crowded with over a thousand passengers and well-wishers, all talking in loud voices to try and make themselves heard above the din. Some looked tearful at the pending departure of loved ones; others joyful at the prospect of a holiday of a lifetime.

As Emily stood at the edge of the crowd, she noticed three police officers diligently scanning the throng. A cold rush of apprehension rushed through her: 'Are they looking for me or simply keeping the crowd in order? Oh golly! I've caught the eye of that one.'

She quickly looked away; it wouldn't do to draw attention to herself, especially in her wedding dress. She kept her head bowed and twisted her shiny new wedding ring nervously, fervently hoping that the policeman did not notice her. Walter, engaged in an animated conversation with his father about America, remained unaware of her anxiety.

When she dared to look up, her stomach tensed in fright as she saw the policeman walking directly towards them. Briefly, she contemplated running away and losing herself in the crowd but her feet seemed firmly rooted to the floor.

Suddenly, he stood towering in front of her: 'You bear a striking resemblance to the description I have of the girl reported missing in Halifax this morning. May I see your passport, please?'

She searched her mind for something to say in reply, then a sudden realisation dawned on her; 'I'm no longer Emily Watson'. She lifted her head as high as she could and looked the officer directly in the eye: 'I am Mrs Lingard. My husband here can vouch for that.'

She spoke slowly and with a haughtiness which surprised her; having never before used her married name, it sounded alien. An authoritative voice behind her interjected loudly: 'And I am her father in law and can confirm that is so.' The policeman looked at James and apologised: 'Sorry, sir. That is not the name I'm looking for.'

Emily watched fearfully as he walked back to his colleagues. Her heart started thumping even faster when she saw him in deep discussion with the other two policemen. What if they didn't believed her? 'Thank goodness the crowd is moving towards the dock, I'll soon be out of police scrutiny.'

The check-in labelled their steel trunks with the cabin numbers on their tickets and whisked them away out of sight. As she approached the gangway assigned to them, Emily suddenly felt faint and asked Walter if he could fetch her a glass of water. He hurried off, leaving her alone with his sister and she slumped down exhausted on someone else's trunk which was waiting to be loaded onto the ship.

Just then, a young ship's officer hurried over: 'Are you Mrs Lingard? You don't look well.' She nodded, too weary from lack of sleep to wonder how he knew her name.

'The Purser has asked me to escort you to your cabin. You've been upgraded to second class as a wedding present from your father in law. Please come with me.'

Annie gave a little clap at this news and pulled Emily up from the trunk. 'Come on – let's go and see what my dad's bought you!' she enthused.

Emily resisted. 'I need to wait for my husband,' she told the ship's officer. But Annie pulled her arm and assured her:

'Walter is with my father and will be sure to follow us as soon as they return'. Reluctantly, Emily allowed herself to be ushered towards the gangway of the huge ship.

The sheer size of the steamer, R.M.S. Scythia, amazed her. Its black hull, white superstructure and single red funnel topped with a black band towered above them as they approached the ship. Only an 'intermediate' 19,000 tonne liner, it had the advantage over larger ships of being able to dock in Boston, their destination in America.

Annie and Emily followed the officer up a gangway usually reserved for the crew to a cabin high above the dock. Moments after they arrived there, James and the best man rushed in and asked: 'Have either of you seen Walter anywhere?'

Emily felt an icy coldness creep over her. 'We thought he was with you!' she cried, and burst into tears. 'I want my husband; he'll never find me here,' she sobbed. Annie gave her a quick hug and left with James and the best man, each promising to find Walter and bring him back – no easy task with so many people milling around.

Five minutes later, Emily still had no news of her husband when the ship's siren sounded. She rushed out of the cabin in a panic, almost bumping headlong into a ship's officer.

'That's the signal for all visitors to leave. We sail in ten minutes; you'll have to go or sail to America with us,' the officer warned and left abruptly to perform his other duties.

Emily ran out onto the deck to search for Walter; surely she would be able to spot him from such a vantage point. 'There he is racing up and down the dock like a headless chicken. WALTER, **WALTER,**' she yelled and waved her arms frantically - but of course it made no difference; the bustle on the quay prevented him from hearing and he did not look up to see her high above him.

Suddenly, she saw the policeman who had questioned her earlier grabbing hold of her husband's arm. He spoke to Walter and pointed at her. She stopped waving: 'What if the policeman has finally realised that I am the missing girl from

Halifax? What if he's about to arrest Walter for abducting me? What do I do, the ship's about to sail? I don't want to go to America without my husband.'

Another blast of the horn and Annie, father in law and best man all made a hurried rush to the nearest gangway. Emily hesitated, should she follow them - but what was happening to her beloved?

She watched breathlessly as the officer led Walter to the gangway of the ship – the same gangway for the crew that Emily and Annie had used earlier. The policeman tipped his hat and stepped back onto the dock. Emily sighed in relief: 'Thank you God, he isn't arresting Walter after all – he's simply trying to reunite the newlyweds!'

Minutes later, the ship cast off to another blast of the horn and, with the assistance of two tugs, pulled slowly away from the quay, black smoke billowing from its funnel. Emily worried: 'I know my Jimmy's safely on-board, but how is he going to find me on this giant ship now that we've been upgraded to a different cabin? I'm all alone in a ship full of strangers bound for the other side of the world.' She walked slowly back to their new cabin and sat on one of the narrow beds to shed a tear and wait, feeling more and more wretched as the minutes ticked by.

The second class cabin, even with its sea view, struck her as far from ideal; two narrow single beds with hard mattresses could hardly be appropriate for a first night of married bliss. The beds, each with a small side table, were separated by a small brown wooden chest of drawers which doubled as a dressing table with a mirror above. A cream carpet square enlivened by an art deco pattern softened the lino on the floor. She hoped her Jimmy would feel the same way about the cabin as she did and do something about it.

***

It took what seemed to Emily like an age before Walter found the small cabin. When he did, she threw herself into his arms and smothered him in kisses. For the first time in their married life they were alone together and she wanted to treasure the moment.

When they finally broke apart, Walter told her: 'When I returned with your glass of water to the place where you were sitting with Annie, I felt absolutely frantic to find the two of you gone! Please promise that you will never leave me like that again.'

They sat on the bed and laughed together at the irony of the policeman who was supposed to arrest them saving the day. Emily finally began to relax but Walter jumped up suddenly as if noticing his surroundings for the first time.

'This cabin won't do at all!' he exclaimed. He gave her a wink, and holding hands they went out onto the deck to look for a steward, but the first steward they saw seemed to be surrounded by complaining passengers. Eventually, they found the same ship's officer who originally guided Emily to the cabin and explained their predicament.

The officer looked thoughtful as he took in the situation: 'You say you're on your honeymoon and on your way to Harvard; I'll have a word with the Captain and see what we can do. The second class is fairly full but the Stock Market Crash destroyed our first class bookings. The passengers don't like to see empty tables; go back to your cabin and I'll let you know what he decides.'

Fortune favoured them with an upgrade to first class, compliments of the Cunard Line. When a senior steward conducted them to their new Cabin Class cabin with a luxurious double bed, Emily felt herself glow with pride at her husband for his success in procuring such luxury. Now they could enjoy a bathroom equal to the very best in Halifax, and lounges, bars and restaurants as opulent as any in London.

Finally, their steel trunks arrived in their new cabin and gave Emily the opportunity of at last being able to change out of her wedding dress. She suddenly felt shy, never before having undressed in front of a man. What should she do? Worse still, she needed help unhooking the fasteners at the back of the dress!

As if sensing her distress, Walter gently turned her around and unhooked the fasteners. Although grateful for his help, she could not stop the flutter of panic in her stomach. She knew what happened on the first night of a marriage, but did not feel ready yet to go ahead.

Walter gave her a light kiss and suggested: 'Why don't you go and relax in the bath for a bit?' She gave him a tight hug, and went happily into the bathroom with her casual navy polka dot skirt and white top, confident that he wasn't about to pressure her for the time being. But as she relaxed in the warm water, she thought: 'What will happen when I get out of this bath? I feel too exhausted and hungry to enjoy sex. I should be happy to be here alone with my husband but is he going to rape me?'

After a while, Jimmy tapped on the bathroom door and enquired in a nervous voice: 'Are you alright in there? I want to go and explore the ship with you.'

What a relief; Emily jumped out of the bath and threw on her clothes before rushing into his arms. They consulted the brochure in their cabin and discovered the extensive facilities now available to them as first class passengers. Then they ventured out together and wandered arm in arm around the ship enthralled by the magnificence of its furnishings.

The steamer boasted a gym with exercise bikes, a swimming pool – not that the pool's décor and size looked particularly inviting on inspection – and shuffleboard. A passing friendly steward told them: 'Don't miss the lavish entertainment available to first class passengers after dinner; dances in the ballroom take place every evening, including a balloon dance and a fancy dress ball.'

As they stood side by side on the deck, they could just make out the outline of England receding in the distance. Emily breathed a deep sigh of relief; no longer worried about her father finding some way of sabotaging their plans. Now they were free and together at last, able to luxuriate at their own pace in one another's company. But she still worried about what would happen after the dinner dance. Would she be able to control her passionate husband?

***

The weather turned cooler as a fresh northerly gale with fierce gusts of wind whipped up the sea, causing white horses to race across it. The huge ship began to roll gently from side to side; not enough to trouble a seasoned sailor but Emily and Walter still needed to find their sea legs. They withdrew hand in hand to the restaurant recommended by their steward.

Neither of them had eaten much all day so they ordered a substantial meal of roast chicken. They both managed the tasty tomato soup enthusiastically, despite its efforts to slurp over the side of the bowl; but then the weather worsened still further and the main course proved more of a challenge. The plates developed a will of their own and seemed determined to slide off the table.

A lady at a nearby table suddenly vomited all over the floor; that in turn caused Emily to feel decidedly queasy. She wanted to return to their cabin but Walter asked her to stay with him until he finished his food. Emily smiled and nodded, all the time wondering how she might make it back to their cabin without being sick.

When Walter enquired if she would like dessert, she shook her head, unable to speak for fear of her stomach's reaction. Seeing her distress, her husband quickly rose from the table and held out his hand. As she took it, she noticed that his hand felt clammy and his face had begun to look a pale shade of green. They stared at each other in panic and staggered along the gangway like a couple of drunks. Both now felt too ill and exhausted to do anything more than collapse onto the bed.

***

Early next morning, Emily woke first and, relieved to be free from her nausea, turned to gaze lovingly at her sleeping husband. Their wedding night hadn't exactly gone as either of them would have wished, but she knew how to make it up to him. Suddenly she didn't feel shy anymore, slipped off her nightdress and pressed her naked body against him. His eyes opened and smiled at her with such love in his eyes that she could feel the breath catch in her throat.

She whispered to him: 'be gentle with me' and he nodded. Then he started to stroke her body gently and kiss her so passionately that all her worries disappeared.

After they made love, Emily rested in her lover's embrace and nuzzled up to him treasuring the moment. The pain of losing her virginity hurt more than she expected, but she thrilled to see her Jimmy looking so pleased with himself. She must not spoil that; her whole future depended on him. Having forsaken her own family, there could be no going back; 'Even my in laws have been left far behind in Britain', she thought.

Walter suddenly announced: 'I quite fancy a game of shuffleboard. I'm not sure how far I'll get with the ship rolling around all over the place. Do you want to come and play?'

Not quite as sure that she had found her sea legs, Emily gave him a fond kiss but told him: 'I'd rather lean on the rail and enjoy the view of the choppy sea. Do you mind?'

When Walter sped off, Emily tentatively ventured out of the cabin and onto the deck. As she leaned over the rail, she sucked in deep breaths of sea air and immediately started to feel invigorated; not only refreshed but emboldened. She needed now to decide how to manage her new husband who came from a very different background to herself. Quite definitely, she would not allow herself to be dominated by him, despite her recent vow to obey him!

As she turned to leave the rail, she noticed a middle aged woman, very smartly dressed in a fitted cotton brown and cream spotted dress and high-heeled cream shoes, staring at her. Unsure what this lady would want, Emily gave her a small smile as she walked past.

But an American voice stopped her in her tracks: 'You're the Halifax girl who disappeared in the middle of the night aren't you?' she accused, looking at Emily closely. 'I've just been reading about it in the ship's paper. It says you were last seen in Liverpool wearing a white dress?'

Emily's hand flew to her mouth. How could her disappearance have made the papers so quickly? The lady looked at her with some concern, 'You look very pale; are you OK?'

Emily felt tears spring to her eyes, though she tried hard to stifle them. Everything was far from OK; in that instant she suddenly felt totally alone, about to face a future in a different and strange country where she knew nobody. All of a sudden her dark red woollen jumper and unfashionable skirt seemed out of place among the first class younger passengers, all smartly dressed in expensive clothes and speaking in posh accents.

Worse, she had just made love with her husband for the first time and wasn't quite sure that sex for her would be as pleasurable as some of the girls on the Halifax switchboard claimed. She found herself pouring her heart out to this perfect stranger, in the hope of receiving some comfort in return.

When she finished, the American lady smiled knowingly. 'The first time with your new husband is always the hardest. You're trying too hard, take your time and relax. You'll see, it'll be alright.'

She gave Emily's hand a reassuring squeeze and walked off elegantly to a group of similarly fashionable ladies standing some distance away further down the deck. Emily could see from the way they kept glancing at her that her predicament would soon spread all over the ship.

She swore under her breath and stamped a foot. 'I must take more care and devote myself to Jimmy, my only true friend in the world,' she confided to a passing seagull.

However, later on in the afternoon, she did take the American lady's advice and made herself relax in Jimmy's arms. She felt more at ease, sufficiently so to give her confidence that her problem with love making would disappear. Both of them were deeply in love with each other and that mattered more than anything else.

As they were getting dressed for dinner in their best clothes, a light tap on their door announced the steward with a note addressed to Walter asking him to report to the purser's office immediately. Emily looked at Walter in despair; she had already filled him in about her disappearance making the newspapers. What if the purser knew too? Nervously, they both went hand in hand only to discover that the purser wanted to check their passports and marriage certificate.

'You **are** the Halifax girl in the paper?' he spoke half accusingly. 'The Captain wants you to wear your wedding dress and sit at his table at dinner tonight. Be there at eight o'clock sharp.'

***

At dinner, Emily found herself seated in the place of honour next to the Captain with Walter on her right. She learned about numerous fabulous places that the ship visited on its cruises and thoroughly enjoyed the meal until, over coffee, the Chief Steward banged the table and called for silence.

The Captain made an announcement: 'Ladies and Gentlemen, we have a celebrity on board, the Halifax lady who you may have read about in today's paper. I am having her installed in the bridal suite. I give you a toast: The Halifax Lady!'

The whole dining room toasted her and then gave three cheers. Emily blushed with embarrassment before a steward ushered them away and showed them to their new suite. He confided: 'Both Ginger Rogers and Rita Heyworth have slept in that bed.'

The opulence of their new bedroom, sitting room and bathroom far exceeded anything either of them had ever previously experienced - all theirs to enjoy for the rest of the voyage. They hugged one another in ecstasy before sampling the vintage Bollinger champagne which the steward poured for them.

When they returned to the dining room to hear Pearl Dorini of the Chicago Opera sing arias from Verdi's operas, they found themselves the centre of attention. A well-known heiress, perhaps the most glamorous and certainly the most bejewelled girl in the room, took Emily on one side and introduced herself.

'Why don't you just call me Pixie, all my friends do?' The size of the pearls in her necklace, the mink stole draped across her shoulders and the diamond broach which she wore made Emily feel shabby and poor in her simple cotton white wedding dress.

'You and I are both about the same size and I'm in the next suite to you. Why don't I give you a couple of my dresses, I never wear the same dress twice. My maid will make any necessary adjustments.'

Emily spent the rest of the week long voyage in ecstasy wearing fine dresses, dancing the night away and making love with Walter. As the liner approached its destination, they bought a guide book of Boston and maps of the city and of the Harvard University campus. Emily studied these avidly making plans about where to visit in their leisure time, whilst Walter combed the newspapers in the ship's library determined to discover all he could about the political and economic situation in America.

The scars from the deep economic depression were still visible, the impact still discussed in the papers four years on from that dreadful day in October 1929 when forty percent evaporated from the market value of stocks and shares in a single day. Share prices had tumbled even further to a mere twenty percent of their cost before the crash. People committed suicide because they could not face their losses or repay money borrowed to buy shares at the top of the market.

Walter commented to Emily: 'Did you know that a quarter of the working age population in America are unemployed; people can't afford to pay their rent and are being evicted and forced to live in shanty town slums. Fierce dust storms sweeping the prairies have caused large numbers of farming families to abandon their land and trek to California. President Hoover sought to protect jobs by imposing high tariffs on foreign goods but the rest of the world has retaliated resulting in the United States loosing many of its export markets.

'I hadn't realised that the amendment to the American Constitution in 1920 prohibiting the sale of alcohol led to a huge surge in illicit supplies by gangsters and an increase in violent crime. It says here that criminal gangs are enforcing protection rackets, prostitution, robberies and other illegal activities.' Emily shuddered. America suddenly lost its appeal as a desirable place to spend her honeymoon.

***

The following afternoon, the ship's siren sounded and the Captain announced over the loudspeaker: 'Land has been sighted. All passengers should please pack their trunks and prepare to disembark.'

As the ship steamed steadily towards Boston shimmering in the September sunshine and gradually filling the horizon, Emily hugged herself in excitement and that lifted her spirits. She couldn't wait to see her new home and experience life at Harvard.

***

Chapter 5

America 1933

Emily knew and cared little about the American economy or politics and she hadn't heard President Roosevelt's address to the nation after his election in November 1932 when he famously pronounced: 'The only thing we have to fear is fear itself – nameless, unreasoning, unjustified terror'. People had lost confidence in the country's banking system and the initial efforts to stabilise the economy and reduce unemployment had proved to be unsuccessful.

For Emily, her dreams of getting away from Halifax and marrying her Jimmy had been achieved, nothing else really mattered. Her first inkling of the life ahead came from overhearing a snatch of conversation between three young American women, about her own age, standing beside them on the deck as the liner neared Boston.

'Do you carry a gun?' one of the girls asked the others. Emily whipped her head around, straining to hear the reply.

'Of course. Most of my friends do,' came the response. 'You need a gun in this country. Boston is less dangerous but when I'm in New York, I often carry three loaded pistols. One in my handbag, but of course that's no use if they snatch the bag. So I put another in a holster strapped to my thigh, but that might not work either if they search me during a holdup. Just in case, I put a third in the small of my back, so I can shoot at them when they run off! And I can shoot straight, my brother taught me.'

Emily turned to Walter and reported the conversation with a catch in her voice as he lent on the deck rail gazing at Boston and trying to make out Harvard. 'What are we going to do?' she gasped. 'We don't have a gun – how are we supposed to protect ourselves?'

He shrugged: 'We're British. We just say that and let things take their course. At least, it should make them think we're unarmed. No point in carrying firearms unless you know how to use them.'

Emily nodded, she did not know how to shoot a gun but it sounded as though most of the American population did; Boston must be far more dangerous than Halifax!

While Walter rushed away to check the arrangements for disembarking and landing their trunks, the American lady, who had given Emily marital advice, took his place at the rail.

'Well, we're coming to the end of the voyage,' she remarked and winked. 'Is everything alright now?' Emily blushed but nodded.

'Good. I'm very pleased to hear it,' she smiled, kindly. 'Where are you going when we land?'

'Harvard. My husband is a Fulbright scholar,' Emily announced, her eyes flashing with pride.

'Good gracious! My husband is a professor at the University. We may be able to help you find your way about.'

Emily thanked her, but felt too embarrassed to encourage a close relationship with someone to whom she had confessed the intimate details of her marriage.

A reporter from the Boston Post came on board the steamer the moment it docked and briefly interviewed Emily, before switching his attention to Pixie, the girl who had so kindly enhanced her wardrobe. Indeed his article headed 'Halifax girl found on Cunard liner' only devoted three lines to the runaways, much to Walter's relief.

Pixie and her publicity man saved the young couple from standing in line for Immigration and saw them onto a coach taking students on the short drive to their hall of residence, 29 Garden Street.

Emily held Walter's hand tightly as the coach wound its way through the traffic towards Harvard. 'Just look at the glorious colours of the leaves on those trees. Isn't this afternoon autumn sunshine wonderful?' she beamed. She felt exhilarated at having at last arrived in Boston and being about to start a new life which would inevitably be completely different from working in Halifax. Would she be able to cope with America?

***

The coach stopped outside a modern tall red-bricked building in Art Deco style and disgorged a dozen or so students who were helped to unload their luggage, register and then directed to their rooms. As strong arms whisked her trunk inside the building, Emily reflected: 'My trunk contains everything I possess in the world apart from the clothes I'm wearing, my handbag and my precious husband.'

The second floor contained a common room where students could mingle as well as two study rooms if they preferred to work outside their own private quarters. She observed that most people smoked cigarettes; some even sported pipes with evil smelling tobacco.

The need to economise had forced Walter to rent a studio on the top floor. This boasted a compact kitchen area fitted with a fridge, oven and sink, a tiny private bathroom and an all-purpose living room/bedroom. A sizeable window gave a breath-taking view over the campus towards the University.

The living room with its polished pine floor measured little more than ten feet square, excluding the area curtained off for the double bed. A small dining table of brown wood with four chairs, a table under the window for studying and a coffee table provided the essentials required by most students.

Emily looked around the tiny apartment, her new home, and realised that she would be sharing with the love of her life a room about the same size as her bedroom in Halifax. More importantly, how could she cope with a double bed only four feet six inches wide?

She opened her mouth to express her dismay to Walter and promptly closed it again when she saw the glow of happiness on his face. 'This is really good, isn't it?' he murmured, putting an arm around her shoulders. 'Our first home as a married couple!'

As they started to unpack their trunks, Walter chatted enthusiastically about how light and airy the room felt: 'It's about the same size as the living room at home in Hebden Bridge – and that room caters for twice as many people!' Emily let him chatter on, she didn't want to spoil his cheerful mood but she had expected something much better.

When they finished unpacking their clothes into the fitted wardrobe and drawers, they checked out the kitchen and bathroom and admired the large patterned rug which softened the otherwise bare floor. Walter flung himself onto the two-seater dark grey settee, motioning to his new wife to sit beside him. There they sat kissing and holding hands until Emily felt her stomach rumble, time to get something to eat.

They made their way down the stairs once again and held hands as they surveyed the food choices on offer. 'Ugh. Look at all those doughnuts, waffles, grab and go triple-decker sandwiches and fast food. None of the cafes on the campus seems to offer anything else,' she complained. They had failed to discover Cronkite or some of the better restaurants but soon found a small grocery store and set about buying groceries for Emily to cook in their very own kitchen.

What should they do after their rather frugal meal of tomato soup followed by cold meat and salad? The unusually sultry weather and a rumble of distant thunder deterred them from venturing out again that evening to explore their new surroundings.

Despite her misgivings, Emily decided to make the best of it. 'We're in our very first home alone together. Let's try out the bed.' Boldly, she took her Jimmy by the hand and led him over to the small double bed. He gallantly went into the bathroom for a shower so that she could get into bed without embarrassment.

He came out to find her naked, covered only by a sheet and looking more beautiful and seductive than ever. They spent the night in one another's arms; a night they would both long remember for their passionate introduction to this new world.

Next morning, Emily felt happy and content; everything would be alright, she had her Jimmy, what else did she really need? She woke first and reminded her husband of his appointment with the tutor assigned to supervise his studies.

He told her all about the interview on his return. 'The tutor is an elderly white- haired man who congratulated me on winning the Fulbright scholarship and suggested that I spend the term writing a paper for publication entitled 'America – The Way Forward'. I am to report progress to him every Tuesday at 10am, when he will offer some guidance and give me a list of the relevant lectures to attend and the books to study.'

From that day on, Walter left their cosy apartment to attend all those lectures, some of which he told his wife were inspirational; and others downright boring. Emily grinned when he described and imitated lecturers who drily read from their notes; and laughed out loud when she heard about others who injected a little humour into their lectures.

They were both fascinated by the way the tutors confidently advocated conflicting views on whether President Roosevelt's New Deal would succeed or fail; economists profoundly disagreed on basic economic theory.

Emily saw how quickly her husband settled into his course and resolved to support him in every way she could. She enjoyed exploring Boston at weekends with the love of her life but had nothing in common with the other occupants of 29 Garden Street, who were all bright intellectuals. Some expressed an interest in life in Britain but this faded when they discovered that she knew far less about London and British politics than they did.

Worse still, she had no interest in baseball or American football any more than they did in the mysteries of cricket or rugby. Moreover, Britain controlled a large Empire scattered all over the world from Canada to Hong Kong and Australia, an Empire on which the sun never set. Historic Boston celebrated the defeat of the British by George Washington and this made Emily feel uncomfortable.

One of the male students even tried to flirt with her and started following her around. She felt affronted and flashed her wedding ring at him. The incident unsettled her and midway through the term, she could hide her feelings no longer.

Too nervous to venture outside the University campus by herself, she had tried to find a kindred spirit amongst the other wives but with limited success. She told Walter: 'I'm lonely here. I've tried to make friends but have absolutely nothing in common with these people. Some of them are distinctly hostile, blaming Britain for raising its interest rates and creating the mess America is now in. Can we move somewhere else?'

Her Jimmy kissed her fondly: 'I'll apply for a transfer to a less elitist University as soon as I've finished the paper which I'm writing. It's already well-advanced. I'll raise the subject with my tutor tomorrow and explain that in the second term I really want to study and write a paper on the workings of the American banking system.'

Emily waited all day inside the apartment for Walter to return, pacing up and down the tiny room; she hoped and prayed he would be transferred somewhere else. When the door finally opened, she sprang up from the settee to greet him.

'Good news!' he announced cheerily. 'Next term we're off to Columbia University New York. It's just off Broadway near the Northern tip of Central Park and I'll have easy access to the banking and commercial heart of the city.'

Emily gulped; New York with all its guns and crime did not strike her as an ideal place to live but at least they would have a change of scene and new acquaintances.

**

Emily purred with delight when Walter told her: 'I've succeeded in obtaining a furnished apartment close to the Morningside Heights campus. It's on Riverside Drive overlooking the Hudson River.'

Her love had gone to great lengths to make her feel more comfortable, even if it proved to be more expensive than he originally intended. He really had listened to her views after all.

They agreed that Walter would use the large bedroom with the king-sized bed as a study during the day. As they stood holding hands looking out of the living room window, Emily hugged her husband in delight. It provided a spectacular view of the river with its ever changing spectacle of ships and boats of all shapes and sizes,

She enthused happily: 'I do love you, I really do. This is everything I dreamed about; we can set up a proper home here.'

Early next morning, Emily studied a guide book on the city whilst Walter went off to introduce himself to his new tutor and explain the nature of the paper that he wanted to write. He reported back to Emily: 'The tutor approved my projected paper but looked decidedly sceptical about the subject. Apparently, the banks here are still in a critical state. It's only two years ago that one of the major banks in New York City suffered a massive withdrawal of deposits causing it to call in loans and ruin many of its customers. Even so, he gave me a list of useful lectures to attend and letters of introduction to three large banks.

'President Roosevelt has rushed through emergency legislation but nobody can be sure whether it will work. A few months ago, the United States ceased to exchange dollars for gold; who knows what damage will result from that.'

Emily supported her husband's endeavours in every way she could by encouraging him to persevere with his article despite the tutor's doubts. She felt particularly proud when the prestigious British Institute of Bankers magazine eventually published Walter's paper about banking in America.

Near neighbours, John and Mary Collins, who lived on the floor above them turned out to be a British couple who welcomed the idea of exploring New York with them. Safety in numbers gave them all more confidence in a crime riddled city. Whilst their husbands were at work, Emily and

Mary went shopping and enjoyed drinking coffee together in a nearby precinct.

John Collins normally worked in the London branch of JP Morgan, a major American bank, and gave Walter invaluable explanations about its organisation and procedures. Unfortunately, their new friends returned to Britain at the beginning of February; Emily missed them terribly and her enthusiasm for New York began to wane when the severe winter weather arrived.

The city often suffers heavy snow falls in January and February, but the 9th February 1934 saw record low temperatures of minus fifteen degrees Fahrenheit; far worse than anything she or Walter had ever experienced in Yorkshire - six people died and scores were treated for frostbite.

No one knew just how long the biting cold would last. Emily complained to Walter: 'I'm starting to feel depressed and am far too nervous to venture out alone. Fortunately, a couple of friendly neighbours pick up groceries for us, so I don't have to face the freezing cold weather too often. It's not just the weather that makes me anxious, I simply don't feel safe walking the streets of New York by myself. Do you remember the girl on the liner who always carries three loaded pistols when in the city?'

A few days later, Walter announced: 'We're moving as soon as I've finished this paper. I think we need to go somewhere warm like California where the sun shines most of the time.' He grinned and they gave one another a big hug, Emily with tears in her eyes.

'The move has been approved because Bank of America based in Los Angeles uses an advanced bank branch system which I want to explore. It employs its own fleet of armoured cars; a perfect excuse for spending my third and last term in America at a University in California.'

***

The end of March found Emily packing up once again, excited to be moving to a warmer and hopefully friendlier place. Her clever Jimmy had secured a postgraduate place at the University of California in Los Angeles (UCLA), which only began to offer postgraduate courses the previous year.

How should they travel from New York to Los Angeles, by train or the cheaper but more rigorous Greyhound bus? Emily pleaded: 'I don't think I can take three nights on a bus.' But Walter argued: 'A bus must be the best way to see America, there will be stops where we can get off and explore places where we would never otherwise go.'

That evening, as a special treat, he took her to see the latest smash hit film, 'It happened one night' starring Clark Gable, which featured romance on a long distance coach. That persuaded her to give the bus a try.

They left New York on a wet April afternoon and by early evening arrived in Philadelphia, a city still reeling from the depression and a strike of textile workers. Emily commented: 'Look how miserable and down-trodden people here seem to be in contrast to the bustle of New York.' Then the bus drove on to a rest stop at Sliding Rock, a beauty spot with a magnificent waterfall, but less appealing at midnight.

The next day took them on through a belt of massive unemployment then away to St Louis on the banks of the magnificent Mississippi river and Kansas City which suffered from all kinds of crime and vice. The bus stayed there for nearly two hours and Emily grimaced at the sight of prostitutes near the bus terminal. 'Look, that girl isn't wearing any knickers,' she exclaimed, clutching Walter's arm.

Their bus began to run behind schedule so cut short the night-time stop at Las Vegas, much to Emily's relief, and arrived at Los Angeles on time. A taxi took them to their apartment just off the UCLA campus. Emily gave him a big hug when she discovered it comprised a decent sized living room with a dining area, and a separate bedroom with a comfortable double bed.

***

Next morning, they explored the campus, thrilled at the sunny weather and relaxed atmosphere. Here, the elitism of Harvard and the pressure to succeed at Columbia were less evident; sports of all kinds seemed as important as academic achievement.

Walter reported to his tutor at UCLA who apologised for the limited number of lectures on offer but did arrange a work placement for him at Bank of America in Los Angeles. This expressed an interest in how branches of the major British banks functioned and agreed to pay him a modest fee if he wrote a paper for them on the subject.

Emily hugged and kissed him when Walter told her: 'The extra money will be a bonus and I've discovered an activity unknown to banks in Britain; an executor and trustee department.' With her encouragement, he made it his business to find out as much as he could about this work and it became the subject of his final article – again published in the British Institute of Bankers magazine.

Once the publishers accepted the article, Walter told her: 'It's time for us to relax and enjoy the honeymoon we have never really experienced. Let's hire a car and go and see the sights! Not just Los Angeles with its film stars but San Francisco, the giant red wood trees, the glorious sandy beaches and perhaps even the Grand Canyon. But before we leave on our big trip, I'd like to check out some of the university teams' activities.'

Emily beamed with pleasure; the idea of behaving like tourists strongly appealed to her. She marvelled at the violence of American football where all the players wore protective clothing and no one seemed to mind if the player tackled did not have the ball.

The sun and scenery and the loving attentiveness of her husband cured Emily's depression and home sickness for England. She told Walter: 'You know, I'd be happy to stay here in California for the rest of my life.'

'I know that you've cut all ties with your family,' he whispered, gently. 'But I still feel close to mine. It wouldn't be right to turn my back on them.'

Emily protested: 'But how can I go back to Yorkshire after everything that's happened? My parents must hate me for disobeying them. They did call the police and must have suffered acute embarrassment given all the publicity.'

Walter reassured her: 'Whilst I would like to return to the UK, I've no wish to live in Yorkshire again. Let's go and explore life in London, the centre of the British Empire; that's where we'll find opportunities in this Depression ridden world.'

He wrote an updated CV emphasising his Fulbright scholarship, his studies at Harvard, Columbia and UCLA, and the published articles. This he sent to the head office of Lloyds Bank in London with a request that they employ him in a position where his studies would be useful. The reply invited him to an interview at the bank when he returned to Britain early in September.

That gave them two months to explore California together. They drove as far north as Eureka, so named because settlers heading for that part of the coast were doomed to perish in the desert unless they found it. On the desert road, a recent sandstorm had exposed the remains of an old covered wagon and the skeletons of the driver and his family. 'This is no place for us,' sobbed Emily. 'Let's get as far away as possible and see the Grand Canyon.'

The vast size and spectacular beauty of the Grand Canyon far exceeded their expectations and they resolved to spend the rest of their vacation exploring some at least of its two hundred and seventy seven miles. Their budget required them to avoid the more expensive hotels but they decided to start at the Maswik Lodge in Grand Canyon Village.

The Lodge, close to the Bright Angel Trail, proved ideal but they were warned to carry bottles of water as the temperature in the Inner Gorge often exceeded one hundred degrees Fahrenheit. Moreover, that it would be unwise to walk more than a mile or so down the steep nineteen mile trail leading to the Colorado River, if they intended to return before dark.

It came as a shock to Emily to discover that they were in Red Indian country: 'Look, the elderly lady over there selling arts and crafts souvenirs has a feather in her hair like a squaw. Ooh, and over there coming towards us is a chief wearing a full head dress. I've read cowboy books, such people are dangerous.'

Walter reassured her that those days were long ago. Even so, they saw bison in the National Park and Hopi Indians roamed everywhere.

***

Much to Emily's delight, Walter suggested: 'Let's start off our journey back to Britain by treating ourselves to a trip on the Southern Pacific's famous Golden State train, which offers a through sleeping coach all the way from Los Angeles to New York.'

The powerful diesel engine hauled streamliner coaches, all painted bright red with a broad silver stripe above the wheels. Film stars regularly took the train to its first stop at Palm Springs and Emily exclaimed: 'Oh look. There's Fred Astaire. I'm sure it's him. I wonder whether Ginger Rogers is on the train.'

The three-day journey seemed endless as it traversed flat prairie after prairie stretching into the distance. Some amenities were provided for passengers including a dining car with a good menu, a coffee shop and lounge cars with comfortable seats.

Although Emily loved the novelty of travelling by train, she found her bunk hard and uncomfortable and missed the privacy to cuddle her husband. One morning after a particularly bad night's sleep, she told Walter crossly: 'In future my vote is that only short train journeys will be allowed.'

Before leaving Los Angeles, Walter had booked passages to Liverpool for them on the M.V. Britannic, a state of the art two funnel White Star diesel driven liner. As Walter had over-spent on their Grand Canyon vacation, they could only afford Tourist Class but were pleased to find that amenities for their class on that ship were far better than they had expected. They did have a private cabin but the bunk beds proved to be just as hard and uncomfortable as those on the Golden State streamliner.

The dining room and bar were spacious and well appointed, the sea calm throughout the voyage and their fellow passengers in Tourist Class more friendly than those on the R.M.S. Scythia. After such varied experiences in the United States, Emily found it much easier to converse with her fellow passengers than on the outward voyage. This time, she and Walter spent every evening dancing to the music of a well-known jazz band.

As the ship moved closer to British shores, Emily couldn't help feeling anxious. She worried: 'I wonder what London will be like. At least the population don't carry guns but big cities are full of people and I know absolutely no one there. Jimmy is so wrapped up in his career that he will be at work all day and I will be left alone. I'm not sure I could stand that. How am I going to make the next stage of our lives together happy and fruitful?'

***

Chapter 6

London

September 1934

On arrival in London, Emily and Walter booked into a hotel in Russell Square and set about finding digs which they could afford. Emily pleaded: 'Choking fog like this where one cannot even see the other side of the road is no place for a baby and we are both trying for a baby aren't we? I would much prefer to live in the suburbs and enjoy fresh air and life at a more leisurely pace.' Her husband appeared to treat her views on the subject as important and she hummed a happy little tune to herself at the thought that she might escape from living in the city after all.

She missed the sunshine of California; London seemed cold and grey in comparison. However, she shared Walter's excitement about his interview with Lloyds Bank now arranged for the following Wednesday. If he received a decent offer, they would be able to build a nest egg and hopefully start a family - her next dream.

When he returned from the interview, she could see from his crestfallen expression that he felt disappointed. 'The two bankers who saw me made it very clear that they were not interested in the workings of US banks.'

Her joy at seeing him subsided; had he wasted his time in America? 'I'm really sorry that your interview turned out to be so disappointing but why did they want to see you?' she enquired as she hugged and kissed him.

'Oh, they did offer me a job in the end!' he smiled. 'Apparently, the Chief Executive liked my article on executor and trustee departments. They think the concept might work here and I've been offered a job in the new department being set up in order to give the bank the benefit of my experience of the difficulties which arise in practice. The salary that comes with the position is materially higher than I expected. I had hoped they would take me on as a trainee banker but when I suggested the idea they declined point blank. We need the money so I swallowed my pride and accepted.'

Emily gave him a big hug: 'It may not be the job of your dreams, but it's a good start. Think what we can do with the money! Now we can afford to rent a house of our very own and start a family. Surely that's as important to you as it is to me?'

She glowed with happiness when Walter kissed her: 'Let's celebrate!' he exclaimed. That evening, they drank a bottle of their favourite Chardonnay and began to plan where to set up home together.

In the Evening News, an article had been published about suburbs being developed around railway stations which provided a frequent service into London for commuters. 'Newly-built semi-detached mock Tudor houses available to rent in Petts Wood are just the sort of thing we want, they are advertised as first homes for newly-married couples,' he suggested.

***

Full of enthusiasm, the very next day they travelled by train to reconnoitre Petts Wood in the sunshine and discovered a huge building site spreading out from the station square. The square itself, with its shops and restaurants, and early phases of the development had already been completed but work continued apace on yet more houses. Woodland surrounded the attractive location, giving the illusion of being deep in the Kent countryside but close enough to London to be commutable.

Having trudged around several properties, both of them particularly favoured a semi-detached house centrally located in Fairway, just a few minutes' walk to the railway station in one direction and a cinema in the other. Apart from three good sized bedrooms, the property boasted a spacious living room, separate dining room and modern kitchen and bathroom.

Emily told Walter: 'The lawn at the back is perfect for a baby; this could be the house of my dreams. I'll make floral curtains for the lounge windows on a sewing machine. One of the bedrooms can be your study and another for the baby!' She hugged herself with excitement; the house seemed to be everything she had dreamed about and more.

As she chatted happily about furnishing the house on the train back to London, she couldn't help but notice that Walter went very quiet; he didn't seem excited at all. Puzzled, she asked him: 'What on earth's the matter?'

He paused for a moment then announced with hesitation in his voice: 'We can just about afford the rent on the house, but will have to wait before furnishing it properly. Let's make a list of the essentials we'll need: a double bed and bedding, a table and two chairs, kitchen utensils, cutlery - -.' The list began to grow alarmingly; Emily bit her lip at the thought of living such a Spartan existence and continued to dream of all the fine things she would eventually want, but kept this to herself.

***

The developers cooperated, pleased to have a bank official as tenant, and within days the young couple signed the lease and moved into their new home. The friendly neighbours helped with the loan of a lawn mower to keep the grass under control.

Emily found weekdays particularly difficult; Walter went off to the bank on an early train and studied for the Institute of Bankers exams in the evenings. She thought: 'Here I am in an empty house, the dreams of all the things I want and not enough money to buy them. The locals in the shops criticise my Yorkshire accent tinged with a touch of American and make me feel like a foreigner. But I do love my Jimmy dearly and must be careful not to do or say anything which would distress him. Why is life so unfair?'

The following autumn, she became pregnant; it should not have come as a surprise but it did. At first, she refrained from telling her Jimmy in case the symptoms turned out to be imaginary. He noticed that she seemed to have become addicted to cheese biscuits of all things and kept complaining of feeling sick.

The disclosure that a doctor had confirmed her condition filled both of them with great joy and he hugged and kissed her passionately. 'I must call my parents,' he announced. 'Are you going to do the same?'

Emily felt a knot in her stomach and burst into floods of tears, burying her head into Walter's shoulder and sobbing: 'I have no problem with you telling your family our news, dearest, but I can't possibly telephone my parents. How can I contact them after all this time given the manner of my parting?

'Still they do have a right to know about my expecting their first grandchild. If I write, father might tear up the letter and throw it on the fire. That's just the sort of thing he would do. I'll talk to my friend Elsie in the morning and ask her to speak to my little sister. I'll never forgive my parents for trying to ruin my life. Thank the Lord that I married you and escaped from them.'

***

Throughout the pregnancy, Emily suffered extraordinary cravings and physical sickness, followed by a painful birth. She tried not to complain; her Jimmy wanted a child every bit as much as she did. The loss of sleep and inability to run her home as efficiently as she wanted made her depressed and the noise made by trains on the main line became more and more irritating.

Things began to get better when she started attending the local ante-natal clinic where she shared her experiences with other pregnant mothers, most of whom also suffered from being left alone for long periods on weekdays. She knew plenty of stories to share about life in the United States and began to be invited to coffee mornings at some of her new friends' homes.

When the baby finally came into the world, Emily immediately began to cheer up; her health dramatically improved and she fell in love with her new son. Cradling the tiny bundle in her arms, she suggested: 'Let's call him Richard, it's a name I like.' Walter readily agreed.

Now she had Richard and the company of new friends, she no longer thought of the days as long and empty. She finally became more settled and her son proved to be the most joyful little companion. When she showed him off to her friends, they marvelled at how much like his father he looked.

Having a third person in the house proved to be expensive; Emily argued with Walter about money: 'I really do insist on the finest cot and pram and luxurious baby clothes. You must understand that I just want the house to be perfect for our baby.'

When Walter told her that they could not afford everything she desired, she stamped her feet and grimaced: 'Why can't you see that my priorities are different from yours? Am I no longer an equal partner in this marriage despite having given birth to your child?'

Not long after Richard's birth, Walter passed his Institute of Banker's exams and the bank promoted him to be one of the select special workers assisting senior management. Promotion meant more pay and the extra money spent on acquiring more baby toys and furniture placated Emily and solidified their relationship.

The house gradually achieved most of the objectives on her wish list; she always believed it would, but seeing the hard earned items of her own choosing delivered to their home provided an enormous boost to her morale.

First came an Indian Agra deep blue carpet square with a dark red border to soften the bare floor boards in the living room. Then two armchairs in the latest Atlantic design upholstered in cotton and a round coffee table with a walnut veneer.

Next, she turned her attention to the dining room and acquired a small table, four matching chairs and an art deco sideboard with a satinwood veneer. To her delight, Walter left the choice entirely to her provided she kept within his budget, unlike her own mother who never experienced such freedom.

Now that she had the place furnished properly, she started to hold her own coffee mornings. The visitors admired her taste and complimented her on the new floral curtains. For the first time since she moved to Petts Wood, she now felt to belong to the community despite their earlier reservations about her accent.

Richard was putting on weight and gurgled happily when she spoke to him. What more could she want? The world in the late 1930s seemed to Emily to be near perfect; and she tried not to listen to Walter when he told her otherwise.

She thought: 'What does it matter if, on the far side of the world, Japan invades China? The atrocities of the Spanish civil war are an irrelevance to us here in peaceful Petts Wood. I know Jimmy worries about the rise of Hitler in Nazi Germany, but why should the politics and fate of such a country so far away concern us.'

When she did discuss the subject with her husband, she always disagreed with him. He became particularly concerned when Hitler annexed Austria: 'It's important that we rearm,' he warned. 'Thank goodness Mr. Chamberlain, our new Prime Minister, recognises that Britain must begin to do so.'

Emily, on the contrary, approved of the Government's pacifist policies. They still made love regularly whenever she wanted and she deferred to his views on nearly everything else, but not in this instance. She told him: 'It's pointless to support rearmament to defend European nations which we have no intention of visiting. Moreover, I'm not alone in holding this view; don't the newspapers say that most of the British population share my pacifism? Don't all my friends agree with me?'

Most of the time, she tried not to engage in discussions on the subject with her husband; it only put him in a bad mood and served no useful purpose. Besides, the baby kept her too busy to take much notice of politics or the world situation. It seemed so much more important to go to the local cinema, once a week on Friday evenings. One of the other mothers, Jennifer Morrison, agreed to baby sit for her in exchange for Emily returning the favour on Wednesdays.

Emily particularly liked Walt Disney's latest film, *Snow White and the Seven Dwarfs*; she hummed the tunes to baby who waved his arms and legs in delight. Her taste in films took her attention away from Europe and back to America. She particularly liked Clark Gable in *San Francisco* and *The Great Ziegfeld;* laughed at Charlie Chaplin in *Modern Times* and danced to Fred Astaire's *The Way You Look Tonight*. Why waste time worrying about war when she could be listening to Bing Crosby singing *Pennies from Heaven* on the radio or Glenn Miller's big band, boogie-woogie or swing dancing music?

***

A few months later, reality struck home when a family of German Jews from Berlin moved into a house a few doors down the street. Jennifer told her: 'The family were forced to flee the country by Nazi Stormtroopers. They were barred from many shops – even food shops – and are lucky to have escaped from the clutches of Hitler.'

Emily countered: 'I agree such treatment is outrageous, but surely what happens in Germany is a matter for the Germans. Britain has no right to dictate how other countries manage their own internal affairs; protest possibly, but certainly not intervene militarily and seek to impose our own morality by force like the Victorians used to do. Surely nobody wants a rerun of the First World War, do they?'

***

Chapter 7

The Storm Breaks

September 1938

When Walter received a further promotion to inspector's assistant at a salary which resolved their financial problems, life for Emily turned around. She had created her own perfect world with Jimmy, toddler Richard and a home of her own well away from her parents, everything that she had dreamed of when she eloped.

She tried to listen when Walter talked about the political situation as he sipped his tea at their homey kitchen table, but still could not fathom exactly what Hitler and his machinations had to do with her.

Whilst out shopping in Petts Wood station square early in October, the caption on the placard of a news-stand caught her attention: 'MR CHAMBERLAIN DECLARES ITS PEACE FOR OUR TIME'. She bought a newspaper immediately and hurried home. The front page reported the Prime Minister's words at the airport, on returning to Britain from a conference in Munich with the German Fuehrer: 'I hold in my hand a piece of paper which bears Herr Hitler's signature as well as mine.'

Emily triumphantly showed the newspaper to her husband when he came home that afternoon: 'I told you we have nothing to worry about! Chamberlain has just declared peace.'

She gasped when Walter shook his head impatiently. 'No Emily, that's not what it means,' he growled. 'I see war as inevitable now the Nazis have taken control in Germany. This country must rearm; the trouble is that most people think like you and consider rearmament will only provoke an arms race. Germany is rearming already and we must do the same; we have to call a halt to the way it annexes its neighbours. The problem is that we are in no shape to take them on. Britain has a strong navy to defend our island from invasion, but the fleet air arm has no modern planes capable of evading the fighters of the Luftwaffe.'

His angry reaction astonished her; what had she done wrong? As her eyes filled with tears, his face softened. 'But what about the Royal Air Force?' she interjected. 'Can't they defend us?'

'The RAF does possess a few squadrons of Hurricanes but the Germans have hundreds of fighters and bombers. They demonstrated the ghastly destructive power of their planes in the Spanish civil war. We comfort ourselves that these aircraft are all short range and little danger to us as long as France stands. If war comes, we will reinforce France, though the French army by itself may be strong enough to hold the Germans in check.'

'So what are you saying? Is war coming?' she cried, afraid now – not wanting to know the answer. Walter took both her hands in his, gave her a peck on the cheek and replied: 'There's absolutely nothing we can do about it but war will come eventually, I'm certain of that.'

Emily burst into tears, partly because Walter had never spoken to her before in such an angry tone and partly because she suspected the truth in what he had said. What were they going to do? Their two year old son started to cry.

***

3rd September 1939

Britain served an ultimatum on Germany which demanded that German forces withdraw from Poland and concluded: '*unless not later that 11a.m. British Summer Time to-day, September 3, satisfactory assurances to the above effect have been given by the German Government and have reached his Majesty's Government in London: a state of war would exist between the two countries as from that hour.'*

On the 3ʳᵈ of September 1939 at 11:15am Walter and Emily listened in total silence to Prime Minister Neville Chamberlain's broadcast to the Nation. In a flat monotonous tone, he announced that the deadline given to Germany to withdraw its forces from Poland had expired. Emily felt fear growing in the pit of her stomach as Chamberlain's voice uttered the words: *'No reply has been received, and German attacks on Poland have continued and intensified.'* The broadcast finally reached its sombre conclusion: *'and consequently this country is **now at war** with Germany.'*

As 'God Save the King', rang out, she couldn't help but see it as a chilling appeal to the Almighty to help a nation so ill-prepared for war. Eyes wide, she looked at Walter, but he simply sighed and switched off the radio. Unlike her, he had expected war and thought about the consequences.

Anger replaced fear as soon as Emily began to realise how much war would change the world – possibly forever. She lost control of her emotions and exploded in righteous indignation as she struggled in vain to hold back her tears: 'One minute it's peace for our time and now he declares war over Poland. How dare he? He's ruined the whole country, condemned us all to live in hell and pay the price. Who cares about Poland? Where is it anyway? What is to become of us?'

Walter shook his head: 'We are helpless victims of events outside our control with little alternative but to struggle on normally for as long as possible,' he sighed. 'What else can we do?'

Emily thought for a moment, straightened her shoulders and gritting her teeth announced: 'There may be a war coming, but we'll be prepared for it. We can stock up with tinned food. I'll make sure the fresh food is kept in our larder, well wrapped or covered by a bowl to keep off the flies . . .'

Before she could continue, a strange ominous wailing sound filled the air. 'It's an air raid siren,' Walter explained, his face creased with worry. Emily watched transfixed as he drew the curtains and jumped when he gently touched her elbow. He told her: 'Quickly, get Richard, get our son and we will hide under the stairs until the danger passes.'

Emily woke the drowsy toddler from his nap and crouched in the small space under the stairs with her family, terrified of being bombed and waited fearfully for the all-clear to sound. She hugged her son tightly, vowing silently to protect him at all costs.

***

1940

Weeks rushed by, and then months, and nothing happened which impinged upon their safety. Emily almost convinced herself that everything had returned to normal; she spent her days with Richard and Walter went to work in London as usual.

The reality of war in peaceful Petts Wood only burst in on her when households received instructions to prepare to defend against bombing. Gas masks, carried in a cardboard container provided, were issued to protect the wearer from potential gas attacks. Emily and her friends accepted these measures with a degree of reluctance, wondering if the masks were really necessary. Forgetting one's mask did not attract any penalty and as time passed the habit of carrying them wore off.

Emily became particularly frustrated about Richard's gas mask. Children were supposed to be supplied with special Mickey Mouse masks, but all Emily could get for her toddler was the standard hot smelly black rubber issue. She struggled to teach him how to put it on, but he hated it; breathing whilst wearing it required an effort.

Ever since the declaration of war, a blackout had been imposed requiring all windows and doors to be covered with heavy blackout curtains sufficient to prevent any glimmer of light from escaping. She tried to argue with the air raid wardens: 'My beautiful floral curtains are perfectly adequate', but they wouldn't hear of it. Sombre depressing plain black curtains had to replace the precious ones which she had so lovingly made.

She worried about Walter walking home from the station at night. Street lights were dimmed, indeed switched off when the sirens sounded, and traffic lights and vehicle lights were hooded to deflect their beams downwards. Trees and lamp posts were painted with white stripes to make them more visible but road accidents dramatically increased. The sound of Walter's key in the door always filled her with a sense of relief on a dark night.

Because of how dangerous it could be, Walter insisted that no-one in the family except him went out after dark. Emily found this bearable during the long days of summer but dire in short winter evenings, even though British Summer Time was extended to last all year round and later supplemented by the introduction of Double Summer Time.

The blackout proved to be of limited value especially on moonlit nights, a Bombers' Moon. The Thames remained visible from the air on most nights, a giveaway for London. Moreover strategic targets like railway marshalling yards, harbours and factories working through the night could not conceal their existence.

And so life went on; it wasn't just the use of petrol, coal, gas and electricity which was curtailed. War brought severe restrictions on clothes and access to basic food supplies such as sugar, butter and bacon in January 1940 and all meat in the following March. The Government gradually extended rationing to include many other foods and even sweets. The amounts allowed were of necessity miserly; one fresh egg a week does not have much impact on one's waistline.

Emily coped with rationing as best she could. The shortages helped to mask the rise in the price of clothes - twenty five per cent in the first six months after the declaration of war but on average only by a third over the whole war.

Some food such as poultry, potatoes, vegetables, fruit and fish were not rationed but supplies were limited. Emily and her friends needed to stand in long queues to feed their families. She tried to be as creative as she could with the limited ingredients, reasoning that dock leaf pudding provided an acceptable substitute for spinach if you were hungry enough, and pancakes made from flour and water could be quite palatable.

Women were exhorted to mobilise themselves and fill the jobs vacated by men who went off to war. Emily and her friends with young children below school age felt relieved that they were exempt from such duties.

She listened closely to Government guidance on how best to prepare food and took part in a 'Dig for Victory' campaign launched in 1939 which encouraged people to dig up their lawns and flower beds and plant vegetables. She pointed out to Richard: 'Look at that poster over there outside the post office, Potato Pete and Doctor Carrot proclaiming that they make good soup,' and tried her best to follow popular wartime slogans, such as 'Careless Talk Costs Lives', 'Make Do and Mend', and the one she said most often to her son, 'Coughs and Sneezes Spread Diseases'.

***

The arrival of an Anderson shelter made a big impact on Emily. One hot summer's day, she watched in horror as Walter and a neighbour dug a pit three feet deep and measuring ten feet by five feet at the bottom of her lovely garden. The earth which they dug out and piled around the hole had to cover the finished structure to a depth of at least fifteen inches, thirty inches on the sides and back.

Their new 'safe' house comprised six corrugated curved iron sheets, three for each side with two steel end pieces, all bolted together to form a hideaway. The resulting shelter had a height of six feet in the centre of the arch and measured six feet six inches long and four feet six inches wide. An earthen blast wall, angled to deflect any blast over the roof, protected the entrance.

Little Richard looked upon the shelter as like having a tent in the garden; but Emily thought: 'Just look at that ghastly edifice ruining the garden. It converts our dream home into a wartime dug out and provides a constant reminder of the horrors everyone expects to come. It's as if we have our own private gateway to hell.'

Later that evening, she debated over dinner with Walter: 'Do you really think an Anderson shelter out in the open is any safer than a dry cupboard under the stairs?'

He admitted: 'Neither alternative is ideal once the bombs begin to fall and the ground to shake. But we have no choice, by Order under the Defence Regulations all shelters must be in place by the 11th June.'

Emily folded her arms and swore to her husband: 'I'll never set foot in that shelter, no matter what happens. I hate the horrible monstrosity, I really do.'

'Let's hope you never have to,' he replied with a catch in his voice.

***

Chapter 8

Danger Strikes

'- - we shall not flag or fail. We shall go on to the end. We shall fight in France, we shall fight in the seas and oceans, we shall fight with growing confidence and strength in the air; we shall defend our Island, whatever the cost may be. We shall fight on the beaches, we shall fight on the landing-grounds, we shall fight in the fields and in the streets, we shall fight in the hills; we shall never surrender.'
(Winston Churchill 4th June 1940)

The true terror and seriousness of the war only hit Emily when she heard Churchill's broadcast. She knew, of course, that Chamberlain had resigned because of the disastrous conduct of the war in France, but Walter convinced her that the new Prime Minister, with his firm determination to win the war, would be just what the country needed.

She knew that her husband tried to shield her from the horrors of the war, but her friends spoke openly about them and this led her to buy a newspaper on her shopping trips, whenever the placards on the news-stand caught her attention.

She read and believed the propaganda that the German invasion of Denmark and Norway the previous April had a serious adverse consequence for the invaders in that their navy suffered heavy losses, weakening its ability to provide adequate cover for a landing on the English coast.

Emily, like other civilians back in Britain, did not at first appreciate the gravity of the attack on France in the truly devastating blitzkrieg of May 1940. Headlong retreat became, according to the propagandists, a series of tactical withdrawals; but when would the front line hold?

The escape of over three hundred thousand men, a major portion of the British Expeditionary Force, from Dunkirk at the beginning of June came to be accepted by the proud but stunned British public as a victory. But their defeated army escaped without heavy equipment and in many cases without weapons of any kind.

The propaganda helped people to believe that the war could still be won, but Emily and her friends suspected from photographs in the newspapers that the British Regular Army, exhausted and acutely short of weapons, would be unable to beat off a sustained attack. What chance would it stand against Panzer Divisions fresh from sweeping some of our best troops out of France in a month?

The fall of France and the rout of allied forces altered the whole shape of the war and for the first time exposed Britain to heavy and sustained air attack. The British Government prepared for invasion, formed the Home Guard from over a million and a quarter volunteers, and set about purchasing arms and ammunition of all kinds, mainly from America and Canada.

Place names were removed from stations and the roads; signposts changed to send strangers in the wrong direction; chaos reigned. Church bells were no longer allowed to be rung; now they would be the signal of a German invasion. If they did invade, civilians were instructed to stay put - not clog the roads like the French refugees had done. These precautions convinced Emily and her friends that an invasion must be imminent.

Where would the Germans land; by parachute or by sea? Perhaps in small numbers at first; the newspapers said they were short of landing craft. Obstacles were placed in fields to obstruct gliders; the whole country went on alert; battle groups were placed in strategic locations.

Everyone became aware that they were all in acute danger, rich and poor alike. This evoked a community spirit which grew when the bombs began to fall. What would it be like to live under German masters? Horrific rumours spread about how they abused women.

Emily and her friends all knew fear but reacted in different ways. She saw her duty clear; she would strive to protect her four year old son at all costs. Some of her friends talked of leaving Petts Wood and moving to the north of England; they asked her what life would be like in Yorkshire.

***

Richard's birthday in June 1940, dawned bright and sunny and Emily with two other young families spent the afternoon in Jennifer Morrison's small garden, laid to grass like her own but not dug up for vegetables. However, this lawn boasted a small plunge pool, too small to swim in but ideal for young children to splash about and keep cool, whilst their mothers sat and chatted in the shade of a nearby apple tree.

Emily went indoors to prepare some spam and tomato sandwiches; rationing precluded anything too elaborate. Suddenly one of the other mothers burst into tears and began to sob uncontrollably. 'What will happen to little Chrissie and me when the Germans invade,' she wailed. 'I don't know what to do.' Her friends stared at her in horror and tried to comfort her but without much conviction or success. 'She's Jewish,' one of them whispered.

'How dare you suggest such a thing as invasion in front of the children,' Emily exploded. 'The Germans invade, indeed; that's defeatist talk. I won't have it.' Defeatist talk was an offence under the Defence Regulations; Britain at war could no longer be the free and easy country of pre-war days and people needed to get used to the idea.

The calm bliss of the suburban tea party shattered; Emily had a terrible feeling that Petts Wood would never be the same again. The party broke up, leaving Emily and Jennifer alone with their children to eat the sandwiches.

***

One weekend a few days later, Walter suggested: 'Let's all have a family picnic tea in the woods a mile or so from home. We'll find a delightful shady open space on a low ridge amongst the silver birch trees, preferably hidden from the path by a clump of rhododendron bushes.'

Where better to spread out a rug and relax quietly, basking peacefully in the sunshine with their small son? Emily remarked: 'Look how near to London we are, yet listening to birdsong on a glorious afternoon as if sitting in the heart of the countryside.'

As they began to pack the cups and dishes away in their picnic basket, Emily bit her lip when Walter broke his news: 'This will be our last visit to these woods. The war situation has worsened dramatically; Italy is now at war with Britain; worse, France has surrendered. London and Petts Wood are now within range of enemy bombers and Britain with its Empire fights on alone.

'I'm going to volunteer for the army, but the bank needs me to stay on for a few weeks. Preserving the banking system is a war priority and to that end the bank's head office is being split up and moved out of London. My team are moving a department to Bournemouth, starting as soon as possible. Why don't you and Richard move there with me? You might even get a summer holiday after all!'

Emily laughed for the first time in a week; she and her Jimmy were going to be together in a holiday resort. But she hated the idea of him volunteering for the army; at least that would not happen for a time so she kept her fears to herself.

The weather could hardly have been better, gloriously sunny just as the winter which followed turned out to be one of the coldest on record. Everyone needed a holiday – the whole country. The realisation that they were almost defenceless gave people the horrors, but a grim determination to struggle on to the end.

Then suddenly and quite unexpectedly, an air raid warning sounded; not the short test bursts of siren people were accustomed to but a prolonged undulating wail of a siren in the distance, taken up by another closer to hand and then a third in Petts Wood itself. Walter and Emily looked at each other in dismay; what were they to do caught out there in the open, not a shelter in sight?

Walter pointed to a tiny dell, not twenty yards away on the Chislehurst side of their ridge. 'Quick. Grab your gas masks but hurry. Leave everything else where it is and keep under the trees. Come on, we'll make for that hollow over there; I'll carry Richard.'

Bushes sheltered them on three sides of the hollow but the London side provided no cover of any kind. 'Never mind; lie flat and keep still. It can't be helped, but we're hardly a prime target,' Walter ordered. Emily cuddled Richard and lay almost on top of him.

Minutes passed, Emily wondered: 'Could it be a false alarm?' She had no way of knowing and fingered her gas mask nervously.

All of a sudden, she heard the splutter of a single low-flying aircraft slowly hauling itself over the hill which separated them from London and heading straight towards their little patch of woodland. At first, trees hid the intruder from view but she guessed from the sound which gradually grew louder and louder that it would be heading towards Petts Wood and the main line railway linking London to the south coast.

All too soon, it emerged at little more than tree top height, the black crosses on its wings and fuselage and the swastika on its tail proclaiming it to be enemy. The sight struck terror into Emily who suddenly realised that the plane was heading directly for them and that the two men in the cockpit, now clearly visible, would wipe out her family if they could.

Black smoke trailed from one of the twin engines of the German plane and the other spluttered erratically. Emily whispered, as if the Germans might hear her: 'Oh look Walter, do you think the pilot will succeed in climbing over our ridge or is he going to crash on top of us? He must have seen the remnants of the picnic which we left behind and know we are nearby.'

High up above, the sun glinted on the wings of a Spitfire watching over its damaged adversary. Emily gripped Walter's arm: 'Look at that fighter, is it going to dive down, machine guns blazing, to finish off its kill? The bullets might hit us.'

'Keep very still,' Walter replied. 'That German plane is finished; the men inside are desperate; they could do anything. It's a Messerschmitt 110, a fighter bomber probing our air defences. We don't know whether it's dropped its bomb load or not.'

As if in answer, somehow the German pilot, hugging the contours of the land, did clear the ridge and moments later jettisoned his last remaining bombs in a final attempt to gain height. Emily heard the explosions and froze, holding her breath as though the Germans might hear. But the planes were gone and the distant rattle of machine gun fire from the Spitfire drove home the message that they would not be returning.

The loud high-pitched whine of the all-clear quickly followed. The mood for basking in the sun evaporated; time to collect their things and go home. The wood now seemed to be a hostile environment; a battle-ground where men fought and died. Emily burst into tears at the realisation that the two Germans were in all probability dead.

Once they reached the main road, she cheered up; the two Germans were enemies after all. 'We're going on holiday to Bournemouth; the sea, fresh air. But when they came to their street, they found Fairway cordoned off and two policemen barring the way. One of them sternly directed: 'Sorry, sir. You'll have to go round; there's been a bomb. The air raid wardens are still combing the area for bodies, three people are missing.'

Walter protested: 'We live down this road just round the bend and need to go home now.'

'Try the church hall down there. They'll give you a cup of tea, and you'll find your neighbours who'll tell you all about it,' the second policeman interjected waving them away. They had no option but to follow his instructions with a sense of growing curiosity and alarm about what had happened.

Emily never liked to make a grand entrance, preferring to slip into a room unobtrusively. This time her arrival received a collective gasp from all their friends and acquaintances, emphasised by Jennifer who dropped her cup and slumped to the floor exclaiming: 'It's them. It is, isn't it? I'm not dreaming, am I? We were told you'd all been blown to bits; are you all right?'

A serious-looking air-raid warden interposed himself. 'Your full names and address please. Come with me and sit at that table in the corner over there.'

He ushered them over to the make-do privacy of his little domain. 'You've put a lot of people to a lot of trouble. Why didn't you report in here half an hour ago when the all-clear sounded?'

Emily could see Walter's cheeks start to flush – a sure sign of his annoyance at the warden's superior attitude. She watched her husband gather himself to give the warden a measured account of their picnic in the woods and the German plane, and felt proud of him for not losing his temper.

'In the woods; in an air raid. That's no way to take care of your family. . .' the warden began but then stopped in mid-sentence, swallowed and flushed.

'I'm sorry, so sorry. I was about to say you should have been in your shelter but it received a direct hit. There's no trace of it, just a huge crater. You'd all have been blown to smithereens; we thought that's what had happened to you. You've all had a lucky escape. Excuse me whilst I call off the search, you are the three people who are missing.'

Emily turned very pale and gripped her husband's hand. 'Would we have been in that shelter? Please tell me we wouldn't, I never did like it. What a place to die,' she sobbed.

Walter looked very serious: 'I don't know, but clearly we weren't meant to die; not this time anyway. It's probably best if you stay here whilst I see if I can arrange somewhere for us to sleep tonight. I'll see what state the house is in and rescue what I can of our things; feel sorry for the wretched landlord. The sooner we're away from Petts Wood the better.'

His sound common sense and calm efficiency impressed Emily. She joined her friends in the hall to hugs, kisses and tears. The bomb could have fallen on any of them and they knew it. They all spent a very emotional evening, especially Emily who realised that she would never again see her home so lovingly created with its floral curtains and the sofa on which she and her Jimmy liked to cuddle together.

Much later, Walter returned in a car with two of his colleagues from work and announced to Emily: 'We must move to Chislehurst immediately where we'll spend the night in Chris Robinson's house, before moving to Bournemouth. The bomb has blown in all the windows at the back of our house, slivers of razor sharp glass lie everywhere and half the roof is missing. It is much too dangerous for you even to look round. I have our valuables and what we really need, the wardens are boarding the house up.'

He turned to the others still in the hall and raised his voice: 'We've all been bloody lucky that there are no casualties. The war is taking my family away from Petts Wood. Good luck to all of you; we shall miss you, but I'm sorry this has to be goodbye.'

Emily kissed and hugged each of her close friends in turn and said a tearful farewell. Jennifer burst out sobbing at the realisation that she would never see Emily again and they both promised to keep in touch and write to one another.

***

Chapter 9

Beside the Sea

Emily and her family arrived in Bournemouth towards the end of June 1940 to find the resort still in holiday mode. She exclaimed: 'People seem to be in denial; they don't realise how serious it is that France has fallen, that German war planes are roaming all over Britain and that invasion could be a reality at any moment. Newspapers are describing the evacuation of allied troops from Dunkirk as a 'victory', but are we truly safe?' Walter's expression said it all as he shook his head and squeezed her hand reassuringly.

Most people in Britain decided to stay at home in the wartime emergency, but Emily's home in Petts Wood had been bombed. Bournemouth seemed to be an ideal refuge, being generally considered of no strategic importance. Lloyds Bank would be paying Walter's expenses to stay in a pleasant three-star hotel at the resort and the hotel manager readily agreed to take Emily and her son for little more than the price of their meals.

She felt particularly pleased that the hotel, located almost a mile from the town centre, was only a short walk from the sea and told her husband: 'This is just the sort of place we need to recover from the trauma of being bombed out of the home I loved so much. I really don't mind all of us sharing a double room facing away from the sea at the back of the hotel. It is only temporary, neither of us knows where you'll be sent next.'

When Walter went off to work each morning, Emily and her son walked down to sun themselves on the beach in the company of a fair number of like-minded holiday makers. One day, she arrived a little later than usual to find her favourite beach quite crowded with mothers and young children below school age. She loved the smell of the sea; it reminded her of holidays in the happy times before this horrible war started.

The sun beat down out of a bright blue cloudless sky, softened by a gentle sea breeze; a perfect summer's day. Swell rolling steadily towards the beach created a soothing effect, a feeling of inevitability; the gentle 'shush' as each wave fell back to make way for the next inducing an aura of calm and peace.

She took her son for a paddle before smothering him in the last of the sun-cream and settling him down to build a sandcastle against the incoming tide whilst she lay sunbathing in the shade of a nearby breakwater. The ripples began to wash the castle away; she watched him struggle to shore it up.

A rustle of excitement from a group nearby caused her to look up from her comfortable resting place; it could not be important but one woman nearby kept pointing out to sea. Emily tried to discover what the fuss was all about, but the sun in her eyes soon forced her to look back to Richard struggling to rebuild the ruins of his sandcastle which now required urgent attention.

'It's coming this way,' the woman shouted excitedly. Emily looked again and out of the haze on the horizon could just make out a tiny speck flying very low above the surface of the calm sea, laboriously making its way directly towards them. Everyone settled down to watch the mystery; a small single seater aircraft flying slowly below the height of the cliffs.

'What is it doing?' Emily wondered. 'Is it looking for something floating in the sea, a mine perhaps or a pilot from a plane shot down over the Channel?'

Nearer and nearer it came, four hundred yards, two hundred. Emily gasped, 'It can't be. The siren hasn't gone!' The woman who first saw the intruder let out a piercing scream.

As all the adults on the beach threw themselves flat, face down on the sand, Emily yelled: 'Richard, come here **at once.** Quickly, get under the breakwater.' He seemed not to hear and stood staring at the plane, now only thirty yards away and no more than forty feet above the water. The pilot, clearly visible in a black flying suit, grinned broadly at the panic created by his unexpected arrival.

To his mother's horror, Richard waved happily at the plane; the German waved back and flew on over the town. Emily rushed forward and clutched her son in her arms as the tiny plane flew over them. The little boy gasped in astonishment: 'Ooh look mummy, it's got a black cross on its side and a small swastika on its tail. Is it German?'

This aircraft looked so harmless, too small to carry bombs and no sign of any weapon; very different from the fighter bomber which had attacked Petts Wood. Emily's relief that her son remained unharmed evaporated when a man's voice behind her yelled: 'Grab that child. He's been signalling to the enemy.'

She turned to see an angry police sergeant, red in the face, running towards them. Thoroughly alarmed, she held Richard tightly and pleaded, 'He's only a child. He doesn't know anything about the war. Please, we're only here because the Nazis bombed our house.'

It took her a good five minutes to satisfy the policeman of Richard's innocence, and she saw all too clearly the look of hatred in the eyes of people around shrinking away from them. Were they in reality German sympathisers, fifth columnist saboteurs for all their innocent appearance?

She marched Richard firmly back to their hotel and told him: 'Promise me you'll never again wave at any Germans. You must come immediately when I call you. That's the last time we go to that beach, but I expect we'll find another one.'

That evening, she told Walter what happened; he looked very grave. 'That must have been a spotter plane taking photographs, but why here?'

'Why did no one shoot it down? It was so low and flying so slowly that they could hardly have missed,' Emily protested.

'Nobody was on guard; nobody expected it. This could be serious; and you young man, next time keep your head down like everyone else,' he ordered Richard, ruffling his hair.

***

Two nights later, they discovered the reason for the spotter plane when, just after Emily kissed goodnight to her son, one siren after another sounded the alarm. They looked at one another and reached for the gas masks; could it be yet another false alarm?

A hotel porter made his way hurriedly down the corridor banging on each door and shouting: 'Air raid. Everyone must go down the staircase and into the cellar. Don't use the lift. Quickly as you can.'

Walter shook his head and remarked firmly to Emily, 'No. I'm not leaving this room; it would be damned uncomfortable spending the night in a cellar crowded with people shivering with fear. Anyway, remember the Anderson shelter which I put up in the garden; if we'd used that, we'd all have been done for.'

Emily pleaded with him: 'Don't be so selfish; think of Richard and me. It would be much safer in the cellar for all of us, you know that.'

'I am,' he snapped back. 'My view is that if a bomb has your name on it, you're dead whatever you do; if it doesn't, you're OK.'

Emily grimaced, frustrated by her husband's belief in predestination. Unlike her, he found great comfort in believing that his fate would be determined by God, whatever he did.

She could not help remembering a placard in one of the garages where they used to buy petrol for their motorbike in happier days when they were courting. It read: 'God helps those who help themselves, but God help them as help themselves here.'

Emily thought: 'I'm an independent woman free to make my own decisions. I would take my child into the cellar, but if Jimmy dies and I live that would be dreadful. What on earth would I do? I can't go back to my parents in Halifax. Can I really bring myself to leave him to his pig-headed fate?'

She discovered that her love for him overpowered her own wishes; it made her stay with him for better or for worse. He really believed in predestination and she resolved to place herself and her son in his hands and pray that they all came through the ordeal safely.

Ten minutes passed since the hotel porter banged on their door and still no sign of enemy attack; Emily began to relax and put Richard back to bed. Then they heard the first explosions - a good way off - no need to panic, but time to pray. A pause in the bombing gave a welcome respite.

Then came a second set of explosions decidedly louder, nearer this time. Things were getting exciting for Emily and her son; Richard pulled the bedclothes over his head.

The third set came close, close enough not only to rattle the windows but to shake the building. Walter reached under the bedclothes and hugged the frightened little boy, whispering in his ear: 'Roll under the bed if it helps. We won't mind.'

Richard shook his head, but Emily did shelter under her bed and tried unsuccessfully to persuade her son to join her. The doctrine of predestination is no good unless you really believe in it, she thought to herself.

The rumble of the explosions quickly died away, only to be superseded by the loud drone of dozens of low-flying aircraft which sounded to be getting closer and closer, heading straight towards their building. She could hear no sign of any fighters intercepting them, no sound of anti-aircraft guns.

Emily felt the dread growing in the pit of her stomach and muttered to herself through clenched teeth: 'We are on our own, just us and the bombers overhead. This is the moment of truth; will we live or die?' She prayed aloud for God to protect her and her family.

The bombers totally ignored the hotel, just flew on and turned back over the sea to France without a shot being fired at them. Bournemouth had indeed been a soft target; it could no longer be a comfortable refuge. Emily crawled out from under the bed, still feeling unsafe. Would the planes load up with more bombs and come straight back? None of the family slept much that night, though Walter insisted that they stay in bed and try to sleep.

Two days after the raid, Walter announced over breakfast: 'The bank requires me to return to London tomorrow; branches around the country are suffering bomb damage. My team is instructed to go into the ruins, open the strong rooms and save what can be saved. With our help, all customer accounts can usually be reconstructed within two days.

'I anticipate that helping to sort out damaged branches will keep me occupied until the bombing eases and then I intend to join the army. I prefer to face the enemy with a gun in my hand and hit back. You must not go back with me to London; that would be much too dangerous. I will be travelling a lot and it will be time to say goodbye tomorrow when I go. I do love you; you know that but duty calls.'

Emily burst into tears at the realisation that she might never see him again, and protested: 'If you really do love me, you can't simply abandon me and Richard here in Bournemouth where we know no one. What am I supposed to do? I'm definitely not returning to my family in Halifax.'

What she wanted seemed to be irrelevant; if her husband must leave her, the protection of her precious four year old son must be her responsibility demanding urgent priority. The Government strongly recommended that all children should be evacuated from London and other potential targets for the bombers. For Emily, that meant leaving the south of England and moving north away from the bombing. She needed to do that and quickly, but how?

She decided to go and live with Walter's family in Yorkshire, if they would have her. Mother and son both qualified as evacuees as Richard had not yet started school, but he would be required to do so in September. Did she really want to go back and live in Yorkshire? That would be quite contrary to her original plans but the war changed everything.

Whilst Walter made the necessary arrangements for their evacuation, Emily tried to bolster her morale with a last visit to the seaside. She needed somewhere quiet to sort out the horrors running through her head. What if she never saw her Jimmy again?

Her choice of beach proved to be a bad idea; when she arrived with Richard at the cliff top, she discovered notices prohibiting access to the sea. Down below, she could see perhaps a thousand soldiers constructing tank traps, laying mines and unrolling miles of barbed wire. Lorries loaded with supplies and some towing guns drove passed her in convoys.

To her, it seemed that Bournemouth had suddenly become aware of its new position on the front line; definitely no place for children. If the Germans returned, they would not find it such a soft target next time.

Clearly she must get evacuated but that proved to be no easy task. Walter registered his wife and son as evacuees on the basis that they were residents of Petts Wood on holiday in Bournemouth. He arranged with his parents that they would welcome the two as evacuees and his father insisted on meeting them at Victoria Station in Manchester when they arrived there.

If only he could escort his family to Manchester, but the rules about evacuation forbade this. In any event, the bank required his immediate help with bombed branches and the war compelled him to do his duty. He made the necessary arrangements with the Authorities, but they warned it could be a while before evacuation took place. Bournemouth itself remained officially a place of safety so evacuation from it ranked low in wartime priorities; indeed residents of the resort ceased to be eligible shortly afterwards when it became designated as a reception area for children from Southampton.

When the time came for Walter to leave, Emily accompanied him to the station and hugged and kissed him until the whistle blew for the London train to depart and they were forced to wave goodbye. Then she hugged and kissed Richard, trying desperately not to upset him but her emotions were far too strong to hide from her son.

***

Both of them returned in tears to their now half empty hotel to find all the holiday makers checking out and returning home. Then began a long and frustrating five month wait for evacuation lasting almost until Christmas, shared with scores of other distressed families. Evacuation may have been exciting for some older children, but no fun at all for their mothers. Indeed, there remained some doubt about whether Emily and her son would be allowed to evacuate at all, which greatly increased the stress she suffered. Bournemouth proved to be far safer from bombing than Manchester, the destination on her official labels.

Emily became acutely conscious of the Battle of Britain waged daily over her head in the autumn of 1940. Where would the Germans strike next? She knew the official view that German plans for the invasion of Britain required the Luftwaffe to establish complete mastery of the air over the Channel and south-east England but now their forces had captured the airfields of Northern France, this seemed almost inevitable. Everyone believed the Royal Air Force to be heavily outnumbered throughout the battle.

The heavy bombing of London began on the 7th September 1940 and intensified over the next fifty seven consecutive nights. This horrified Emily who now really did begin to worry about Walter; she had heard nothing from him for several days. Desperate to discover what dangers her husband faced, she developed a passion for news about the war.

Official media were trying to hide the true facts, but so many people experienced the reality on the ground that she gleaned enough information to gain an impression of the truth and it frightened her. Knowing Walter's aversion to air-raid shelters, she lived in constant fear that she would never see him again. She listened in horror to the six o'clock news every evening and winced at the reports of casualties. If he did not die, he might be burned or blinded.

Her anxiety increased because of the difficulty they found in communicating with one another. Walter had no fixed abode, but in an emergency could be contacted through Lloyds Bank's head office. She would use this on her arrival in Hebden Bridge but not for the love letters she penned daily but could not post without an address. He lost the ability to make private telephone calls and the post became unreliable as sorting offices were destroyed.

Emily spent her days trying to teach Richard how to read and write - conscious that he should be starting school - and worrying about what she would do if she lost her Jimmy.

By early December, the Authorities decided that the pressure on the railways had eased sufficiently to allow refugees to travel again and Emily and her son were at last instructed to report to the railway station.

***

Chapter 10

Evacuation

Emily arrived at the railway station with official refugee labels entitling herself and Richard to third class rail transport to Manchester but no instructions on how to get there. Her husband had made it very clear that London must be avoided at all costs and petrol rationing made travel by car impossible. Coaches, or *charabancs* as they were called, existed but were requisitioned to move troops to strategic positions in the event of invasion.

That left the railway using a west coast route to Manchester where Walter's father, James, would pick them up by car. Travel by train proved no easy matter for Emily; no one she knew in Bournemouth wanted to go to her destination, especially as Manchester itself with its docks and heavy industry had become a prime target for enemy bombers.

The apologetic Station Master advised her against travelling via Southampton which regularly suffered heavy bombing. He equally advised against going through Bristol for the same reason. Instead, he recommended a local service to Yeovil where she should be able to board a train to Bath.

She realised that, after all the time she and Richard had spent wandering hopelessly from platform to platform, he wanted to get her out of his station, a need which she came to share as darkness fell with no train in increasingly damp chilly weather.

Eventually, she and her son boarded a succession of trains which crawled along to their destinations; frequently diverted into sidings or around loops in order to give way to high priority military traffic. The railways had become a strategic target for sporadic bombers; no hope of trains running to timetable; the war made it too dangerous to publicise their itinerary. Travellers were forced to wait patiently and take their chance when a train came.

None of the stations displayed names, an emergency measure designed to confuse the enemy, which certainly confused Emily. She became hopelessly lost, the more so as a baby crying in her compartment sometimes made it impossible to hear information being shouted by porters.

It took nearly three hours to reach Yeovil where she needed to change trains. The connection for Bath already stood on another platform and she and Richard ran to catch it. Shortly after the train left the station, Emily's heart sank when an air-raid warning sounded.

The train raced for the cover of a distant tunnel, screaming to a halt when safely inside and remaining there for fully half an hour. The stench of smoke and steam from military expresses travelling in the opposite direction added to Emily's misery and made her feel sick.

She desperately wanted to seek Walter's advice about how best to travel when she reached Bath, but had no means of contacting him. She knew he worked on bomb sites during the day and sheltered, like thousands of others, in the London underground at night. The realisation that she could not contact him made her aware of just how much she had come to rely upon his support and guidance.

She sat up straight and told herself: 'I must be strong and persevere with my complicated itinerary. War has made life difficult for everybody; I must fend for myself and Richard, not collapse helplessly in floods of tears.' Even so, the delays were frustrating and she could not prevent an occasional tear running down her face.

Her fellow passengers tried to cheer her up: 'You've got your destination on the labels, it really doesn't matter how you get there as long as you and the boy are safe! You'll recognise Bath when you see it.' But Bath meant nothing to Emily and she felt no real desire to go there. Geography had never been her strong point at school; whereabouts was it in relation to Manchester?

The food she brought with them for the journey did not last and compelled her to rely on railway buffets. These sold stale sandwiches and rock-hard buns, which Richard washed down with water and Emily tried to swallow by drinking a substance euphemistically called tea, but bearing little resemblance to her usual type. She reflected bitterly that nothing felt or tasted the same anymore.

When the local train finally chugged into Bath station, Emily followed a number of other passengers over to the buffet where three bad-tempered harassed tea ladies struggled to cope with the mass of potential customers clamouring for attention. They stood behind a long wooden counter bearing two large 'tea' urns, one at each end. This barrier provided some protection from the abuse about slow service and the appalling quality of the food being hurled at them by customers 'lucky' enough to have been served.

Some soldiers amongst the throng crammed into the tea room wolf-whistled admiringly when they saw Emily but did push a space for her at the counter and called for her to be served. She paid for her purchases of stale tomato sandwiches and bottled water and hurried out with Richard, vowing never to return.

The two of them eventually arrived at Crewe after their train suffered a frustrating two-hour wait outside the station for reasons she never discovered. The station still functioned despite bomb damage from a severe air raid a few weeks earlier.

Exhausted, Emily climbed out of the train with her luggage and clutched Richard's hand as she searched for the right platform to catch the Manchester train. The enquiry office revealed: 'Manchester suffered heavy bombing last night and the area around Victoria station is still ablaze with numerous fires, many of which remain out of control. All services to Manchester have been suspended until further notice.'

Emily in desperation telephoned Walter's father who told her: 'You stay put in Crewe at my expense until the Manchester station reopens and then try again. Meanwhile, I'll remain in Hebden Bridge and rely on my contacts in Manchester to let me know when services are restored.'

***

Emily and Richard, desperate to leave Crew before it suffered further bombing, caught the first train to reach a devastated Victoria station. The square outside the entrance, still on fire with an all-pervasive smell of burning, teamed full of fire engines, police and air-raid wardens who swarmed everywhere.

A policeman came over to Emily and demanded: 'What are you doing coming to a fire swept hell like this and bringing your little boy with you? Surely you are not intending to go sightseeing – there could be unexploded bombs. This area is unsafe, you must leave it immediately. I suggest you make for the Victoria Hotel over there.'

Emily recoiled at the complete and utter devastation which confronted her. She learned that an intensive incendiary attack illuminated the city prior to bombardment by increasingly heavy calibre high explosive bombs and land mines, which blasted buildings apart all over the city centre. The prestigious Victoria Buildings had collapsed into Deansgate, tangling the overhead tram lines under piles of debris. A bomb which fell close by had ripped the fronts off a whole row of terraced houses down one side-street.

Uncontrollable fires still burning fiercely spread over a wide area getting ever redder and brighter as the flames took hold and spread from building to building. A mass of flames engulfed a whole row of doomed five-storey warehouses; every window alight from end to end and top to bottom with fire blazing skywards through rooves which had collapsed onto the floors below. Emily would never forget the sight of that inferno which threw off a heat so intense that firemen sprayed water on nearby buildings creating white steam rising into the smoke-filled sky.

The sound of buildings collapsing or being torn down all around and the stench of burning rubber tyres on wrecked vehicles increased the drama. Debris, broken glass and fire hoses littered the roads. Many side streets had been made impassable by large coping stones which had fallen from the top of buildings and by beams of blackened wood jutting out of piles of broken bricks.

Countless fire tenders sprayed water on the burning shells of buildings; those not still on fire being left as piles of smoking and smouldering rubble. From snatches of conversation which she overheard, Emily realised that the dazed and shocked population seemed to have developed a comradery, showing caring and kindness to each other, and even cracking jokes in their determination to live each day as it came.

She heard a fireman call over to one of his colleagues: 'Free beer at the hotel bar when we come off shift tonight, thanks to Adolf.' Another voice announced: 'The big stores in the city centre are giving away fire damaged stock; some real bargains if you take them away.'

Emily felt no such sense of community spirit; she did not want to join in, feeling a need to get away from Manchester with Richard as fast as possible. She reflected that much of London must be like this; the thought of her Jimmy living and working there made her feel ill.

James had learned about the station reopening and found them as they made their way through the rubble towards the Victoria Hotel: 'It's good to see you are both safe. I must apologize for parking my car some distance away but the roads near the station are closed. However, I've booked lunch for all of us at the hotel over there; it's one of the best in Manchester.'

Emily protested: 'I'm in no fit state to patronise such a grand establishment'; but James ignored her and kept repeating: 'We must hurry or the restaurant will stop serving.'

When they finally reached the restaurant, it proved to be virtually empty. Clearly the bombing created so much devastation that very few wished to remain anywhere near. Despite being ravenous, the sound of collapsing buildings being torn down certainly killed Emily's appetite.

One of the quirks of rationing permitted food to be served in restaurants without using coupons, but Government regulations imposed a maximum price of five shillings per person. The Victoria continued to produce relatively exotic meals but with slices of melon cut wafer thin.

Over lunch and in the thirty minute car journey to Hebden Bridge immediately afterwards, James quizzed Emily about her life in America. The memories came flooding back and acted as a tonic lifting her out of her depression. An exhausted Richard fell asleep as soon as the car left Manchester.

**

Hebden Bridge saw little of the war; occasionally the sirens sounded but enemy bombers sought more worthwhile targets in neighbouring towns. The evacuees climbed the steep hill to James' house and Emily received something of a heroine's welcome. However, she and Richard were to sleep in the attic and the stairs to that were steep and narrow.

The attic filled the roof space of the terraced house with stairs giving access in the centre of the room. Two rugs partially covered the bare floor boards and the furnishings were limited to a single bed and wooden chair under the sloping eaves on each side. At least it felt dry but, once the sun went down, the lack of any heating made it cold and uncomfortable. Ada urged Emily to check that she had enough blankets.

Emily, as a privileged guest, was ushered into the front room with its brown three piece suite, radio and piano. James enquired politely: 'Can you play the piano?' 'Oh yes,' she replied, 'but the music by Handel which is open is too difficult for me to play unrehearsed.'

'We don't mind; play something you know,' James told her. She did; a piece of Boogie-Woogie learned in the United States and played fast and competently. To Emily, this music signalled her defiance. Grimly determined to start as she meant to continue, she made the decision to show her independence and not demean herself to grandfather's puritanical regime.

Ada gave them tea, comprising home-made bread and jam and a cup of tea for the adults, milk for Richard. Milk delivered in churns direct from the local farms seemed to be plentiful in the area throughout the war. After tea, Emily expressed herself to be exhausted and suggested a bath then bed.

'Sorry, there is no hot water for a bath. There will be in the morning,' Ada instructed firmly. Emily thought: 'Life in Yorkshire seems clearly more primitive than in Petts Wood or Bournemouth', but at least she and Richard were safe, weren't they?

'Do you have an air-raid shelter?' she enquired as she turned to go upstairs. They showed her the door to the cellar.

That night Emily lay tossing and turning unable to sleep on the hard uncomfortable bed in the freezing attic. Her son snored contentedly but that did not help. She realized that in this household grandfather ruled and she needed to live her own life free from his control; she had married and deeply loved Walter, not his dictatorial father.

Next morning, she came downstairs to find that James had already gone to work an hour earlier and the breakfast things were being cleared away. Richard slipped on the top step and fell head over heels in a double somersault to end sitting yelling on the bottom step.

Ada slapped him hard across the face and, to his mother's astonishment, told the child: 'Think of the neighbours and stop making that terrible noise.' Emily reflected bitterly that this consideration for others did not apply when James daily practiced his tenor solos and Annie her scales.

Richard complained that the slap had made one of his teeth come loose. Hebden Bridge lacked a qualified dentist at that time and, before Emily could stop her, Ada tied a slip knot in a piece of thread and gently slipped it over the offending baby tooth. She then tied the other end of the thread to the handle of the open hall door and slammed the door shut.

Sight of the extracted tooth, presented to its owner to place under his pillow for the tooth fairy, caused Richard to slump into the nearest chair too shocked to react and his mother rushed over to examine his mouth and protect him from further violence.

Relations between mother and her mother-in-law suffered serious damage as a result of the incident and other problems soon emerged, the house being really too small for five people. In particular, the bathroom contained the only toilet and Ada insisted on the front room remaining in pristine condition in case unexpected visitors called.

The extra ration books which Emily brought with her enabled a small joint of beef to be purchased for Sunday lunch with roast potatoes. Ada used every scrap of meat, the fatty juices carefully poured into a bowl to be eaten subsequently as bread and dripping and any left overs passed through a mincer to make minced meat. Similarly, the neck and bones of the Christmas turkey were boiled to make turkey soup. This household did not starve but followed the wartime slogan 'waste not want not'.

When James returned home from work, he shocked Emily by announcing: 'I regret that your stay in this house can only be temporary, extending over the Christmas holidays. However, I do own a disused farm cottage in Pecket Well which is being renovated for you. My workmen are replacing the rotten timber floor with concrete and generally making the place habitable. You and Richard should be alright there and I'll introduce you to the farmer who lives next door and visit from time to time to see that you're OK.' He took care never to suggest any degree of comfort, much less luxury.

Emily desperately wanted the work on that cottage to be finished; Richard needed to start at the village school as soon as possible after the Christmas holiday. Meanwhile she continued to do her best to teach him how to read and write. Her offers to help Ada in the kitchen or with the washing and shopping seemed to be resented; these were grandmother's territory and no one else in the family dared to interfere.

But would she really be alright stranded alone with her young son in a tiny village where she knew nobody? Ada did her best to make the evacuees comfortable, but stopped short of begging them not to leave.

***

Chapter 11

Farm Life

As James drove Emily and Richard to their new home, he explained: 'The village straddles the main road from Hebden Bridge to Keighley at the top of this steep climb and runs just below the crest of the hill. Fertile meadows surround it and you'll see rolling hills to the west which provide superb views from the cottage. Higher up the hill, the fields give way to heather clad moors stretching mile after mile to Howarth and Bronte country. Pecket, as the locals call it, does have a small mill now taken over for secret war work.'

Even in wartime, the village appeared to Emily to be a place of peace and tranquillity with sheep and cattle grazing in the fields. Listening to James talking, she wondered whether the mill might be producing some vital part for the Hurricane fighter, but good sense forced her not to ask; 'Careless talk costs lives' as the placards drummed into everyone rang in her ears.

James continued: 'Just beyond the village, a stone paved pack horse track drops down the steep hillside to Crimsworth Dean and Hardcastle Crags where you've been many times with my son. The river at the bottom of the valley has spawned a series of old water courses and ponds once used to store water for Gibson mill and the other weaving sheds further downstream. Lumb falls with its twin waterfalls and an old packhorse bridge is idyllic in summer and autumn and a haven for wild life; Midgehole can live up to its name!'

Emily laughed: 'That's one place I'll give a miss.' It crossed her mind that she and Richard might very well visit her own special place near the Crags where Walter proposed to her. She missed him terribly and hoped that being there might help to bring back memories and make her feel closer to him.

Pecket's amenities included a pub called The Robin Hood Inn and a general store which included a tiny sub-post office. The place also had its own village policeman and a small school with two class rooms. Nothing more, no church or chapel, but hill farm after farm stretching all the way to the moors in the distance.

They arrived at their new home and James helped Emily to unload the sheets and blankets which Ada had supplied and showed her around. He hugged her goodbye with a: 'I must go now but I'll tell the people at the farm that you've arrived. Contact the farm in an emergency and they'll be in touch with me.'

***

The cottage, which used to belong to the neighbouring farm, stood down a short lane on the edge of the village closest to the moors. Its tiny garden backed onto the farm yard and the smell of manure could be overpowering when the wind blew from the south.

The accommodation comprised a small living room heated by a log fire, one bedroom and a minute kitchen. It had no bathroom, just a tin bath for use in front of the fire. However, it did possess electricity, if no power cut intervened, and running water from the nearby reservoir. Unfortunately, the granite stone walls and concrete floor lacked a damp course. It rains a lot in Yorkshire, the winters are biting cold and the cottage seemed to suck in the damp; everything in it became wet and that made it feel very cold if the fire went out.

The farms which she could see from her vantage point reminded Emily of Wuthering Heights as portrayed by Emily Bronte, creepy on a dark night. She noticed that there were no street lights in the village to be blacked out! Telegraph poles carried the electricity cables and when the wind got up, it would howl through the wires like a wailing banshee. She vowed not to go out after dark, except to the toilet in a hut in the small garden – a trip which would be freezing cold and scary.

In her haste to leave Hebden Bridge, Emily never anticipated how badly the bare damp cottage would affect her standard of living. February 1941 turned out to be one of the harshest in living memory; a few days after she moved into the cottage, the pipes froze solid. Worse, during the night deep snow drifts covered the door and windows, isolating her from the farm and the rest of the village. Without a telephone, she and her son were cut off from humanity in an isolated spot without any friends and only a limited supply of food, a real test for Emily's character.

She felt lonely and devastated but wiped away her tears and shrugged off her dismay; these conditions were nowhere near as bad as she had experienced in New York on her honeymoon. She decided to dig her way through the snow to the farmhouse nearby, if only she could force open the cottage door.

Her plans for digging were interrupted by Richard: 'Ooh! Look over there at that long tail sticking out from behind the oven.' At the sight of the tail, she let out a loud scream and jumped onto a chair. 'Don't touch it. It's a rat. Hit it with the broom and drive it away.' But the rat disappeared through a hole in the wall before the little boy could reach it.

The incident energised Emily who forced the door ajar with a strength she did not know she possessed and began to dig frantically. Once outside and through the drift, she saw the farmer, Jess Irvine, digging a path through in her direction. He waved cheerily: 'Why don't you pack what you need and join my family in the farm house until the weather improves? I heard you scream just now about the rats but that's one worry you can forget. One of my dogs wins rosettes for rat catching and will check out your cottage whenever you want.'

She readily accepted his invitation and the warmth of the farm kitchen with its roaring log fire in a huge hearth and the friendly reception from the farmer's wife, Elsie, soon brought a smile back to her face. 'You sit down here in the oak rocking chair and rest whilst I put the copper kettle on the stove and make us all a cup of tea. I've been meaning to call on you before but we've all been so busy. We need all the help we can get on the farm, particularly when the lambing season starts.'

A large solid wooden table at which a Land Girl laboured away making cheese filled one end of the room. The farmer explained: 'Weather conditions are too severe to deliver the churns filled from milking our cows this morning, hence the cheese making. How about you giving us a hand with lambing, the poultry and cheese making on a part time basis in return for logs, eggs and milk?'

Emily thanked him: 'I'd love to help out. Delivering lambs is something I know nothing about but I'm sure there is lots I can do to help.' She sat back, drank her tea and admired the dark oak welsh dresser, the earthenware pots on a shelf above it and the black leaded grate with its brass poker and fire tongs. Two rugs on the tiled floor made this predominantly working environment feel more homely.

***

As soon as the freezing conditions allowed, Richard started school and Emily registered for war work as required by the Defence Regulations. She volunteered to work on the farm but, in view of her time at the Halifax Building Society, found herself allocated to assist part time in the village post office as well as with the farm.

Once she began work at the post office, she soon came to know many of the villagers but had little in common with any of them. With few exceptions, they never went to Halifax, even though only eleven miles away, and seemed to regard it as another world. In their eyes, she was a foreigner, her Yorkshire accent having been diluted with a mixture of American and Southern English.

The post office gave her access to its telephone and enabled Walter to call her when bombing and his increasingly arduous work on bomb sites permitted. In one such call, he told her: 'Finding the dead bodies of defenceless civilians buried under rubble in bank branches sickens me. The buildings are supposed to be cleared before I go in, but at the height of the blitz the authorities have become overstretched. I'm OK but intend to join the army just as soon as I can.'

Emily begged him: 'Please don't volunteer for the army; think of Richard and me. I really don't know what I'd do if anything happened to you,'

She struggled on living in the village without complaining, but with no form of leisure activity. She worked hard all hours as did many others in the same position. The need to keep the village post office open and look after her son, restricted her activities on the farm and she never became a Land Girl. Their duties included milking cows, ploughing and gathering crops and even catching rats.

Emily met several of the Land Girls at harvest time. Indeed, all the villagers (including five year old Richard) were mobilised and given implements to cut corn growing in fields too steep for agricultural machinery.

On hot summer's days, the children were sent home from school and instructed how to use a small curved blade about a foot long. The men carved great swathes in the corn with two handed scythes; the children followed them at a safe distance, cutting any tufts they might have missed. The cut corn was then forked onto a horse drawn cart and taken to a threshing machine in the farm yard.

***

The village children made their own way to school unaccompanied; mothers of school age children were required to work and petrol rationing made it impractical to drive them to school. For Richard, this entailed a walk of half a mile or so from one end of the village to the other.

Fortunately for Emily he could manage this, but on one occasion as he told his mother: 'A village dog bit me on the way to school. I arrived covered in blood stains. By the time school ended, the dog had been caught and shot so that all of us could walk home safely.'

Like many other evacuees, they endured life in a closed community, strangers from a different background imposed on the others by an accident of war. Naturally, an attempt was made to bully Richard, but he knew from his father how to punch putting the full weight of his body behind each blow.

One spring day he returned from school covered in mud and bruises and told his mother: 'As we were assembling for school, the leader of the village boys in my class brandished a toy knife carved out of wood and boasted to his friends that he would demonstrate how commandoes killed the enemy. I pretended not to have heard and turned my back but listened intently to events behind me.

'The boy crept up with the knife brandished above his head and as he plunged it down, I swung round and hit him in the stomach so hard that he dropped the knife and doubled up in tears clutching his stomach. The teacher simply said that would teach us not to fight in the playground.

'After school, the boys challenged me to a fight, one against one. We went to a field out of sight of the school; their leader began to punch me and I defended myself. Both of us were about the same height and weight and very evenly matched, but it soon became clear that his punches were weakening; he struggled on bravely as long as he could but in the end broke away and ran home in tears.'

From the state of her son, Emily doubted whether he had been the victor and ordered him into the bath while she washed his clothes, all the time wondering about how she could protect him from bullying in a hostile community.

Suddenly, hearing a knock on the door, she wiped her hands with a towel and opened it to find an angry blond woman about her own age in overalls glaring threateningly at her: 'You keep that son of yours under control, coming here to our village and upsetting everybody. How dare he beat up my boy like that? You've not heard the last of this.' With which the stranger turned away and marched off before Emily could say anything. She looked at her son with new respect; he really had won the fight, perhaps he could stand up for himself after all.

The day after the fight, she frowned when Richard told her: 'This morning in break, the leader of the village boys told me that the gang would be mine if I wanted to lead it. I simply replied: 'No, they're your friends and it's your village. I too would like to be your friend and will back you up with the others. Let's have a truce'. He readily agreed and now we're all friends together.

Richard's new friends showed him hideaways in the woods and short cuts through the fields, even braving the local bull field together. The contours of the hill prevented the whole field being visible from the style which gave access, and more than once the boys were forced to run for their lives when the bull came thundering over the ridge.

Shortly afterwards, Emily herself began to be accepted by the villagers, her cottage being every bit as cold and damp as the others and her lifestyle no better; indeed, being down a lane on the edge of the village, she was even more isolated than most.

Emily took her young son to a dance organised by the school for parents. This proved to be far more boisterous than she expected introducing her to such local favourites as *Bumpsy daisy* and *Chickery Chick Chela Chela*! She gritted her teeth and joined in the fun, at least it gave her an opportunity to get to know the two teachers.

One sunny day, the farmer's wife asked Richard to take her pet black retriever for a walk in the woods down Crimsworth

Dean. 'Be sure to keep tight hold of the lead. If you get lost just shout "home" at Blackie and she'll bring you back.'

Richard reported his adventure to Emily: 'We set off down the packhorse trail on what promised to be a super adventure. Blackie is a strong young dog and pulled hard on the lead forcing me to run in order to keep up with her. Once we reached the bottom of the valley, I sat on a tree stump to recover my breath.

'Suddenly, a partridge swooped low over the ground in front of us. The dog took off after it before I could move and tore the lead from my hand. Worse, the bird flew on low over a mill pond covered with a carpet of leaves and Blackie sprang to grab her prey, only to fall into the water with a huge splash.

'The dog could swim strongly but the deep water prevented her from climbing out. I called for help but no one heard; so I found a stick and Blackie swam to me. Fishing the lead out of the water, I pulled and the dog tried to scramble out over the dam wall but without success.

'We tried in two or three places before I eventually discovered one where Blackie succeeded in finding a purchase and jumping out. As a reward, she shook herself vigorously drenching me in filthy water. That's why I'm so wet. I shouted 'Home' and here we are.' Emily, who had begun to wonder why they were away for such a long time, simply ordered him into a hot bath and straight to bed!

Richard enjoyed one big advantage over the other children; Emily had taught him how to read and write and do simple sums before he even started school. The teacher constantly complained that she could not read his handwriting. One day she offered a prize for the neatest copy of a short text - a pencil, sold to raise funds for French soldiers who made their escape to Britain, which bore some writing in French and a tricolour at the end. Richard wanted that pencil and really concentrated on the task in hand producing immaculate copper plate handwriting to the teacher's utter astonishment.

At school, all the children were given a dark blue card issued by the Royal Air Force on which were printed black silhouettes of eight aircraft; four British and four German. If they saw any German planes, they were instructed to count how many of each type and inform the nearest adult, who should immediately tell the police.

A few days later, the village from its vantage point near the crest of the hill did see a flight of German bombers lumbering noisily and painfully slowly across the skyline in the direction of Leeds. The village policeman made it very clear in unmistakeable and unprintable terms that he did not need the children's assistance in counting them!

For Emily and her son, the summer of 1941 marked a big improvement on the cold and damp of the previous winter. James would come at weekends and drive them to local beauty spots to enjoy spectacular views over the moors. In places, they could see for miles with no sign of human habitation - just hills, granite outcrops and the smell of fresh clean air and heather.

The local farmers grazed their sheep on the moors in summer, using sheep dogs to round them up. That summer, one flock from Jess Irvine's farm were panicked by a low flying plane and committed mass suicide by bolting over a cliff. The farmer reported his loss to the Ministry of Agriculture who told him not to worry; they would collect the carcasses and have them manufactured into corned beef, a product which formed part of the wartime meat ration.

After school, Emily allowed Richard to listen to the radio; Children's Hour, in practice never more than half an hour in this period of the war. He particularly liked Toy Town which became his firm favourite with Larry the lamb, Dennis the dachshund and Mr Growser the grocer. Emily too had her favourite programs, she particularly enjoyed listening to Music While You Work which broadcast jaunty popular music such as 'Run, Rabbit, Run', played at a fast tempo, which James told her speeded up production in the factories.

She refused to let Richard hear the news in case it gave him nightmares, though she would listen to it once he fell asleep. She felt desperate for information about events which might affect her Jimmy. Occasionally, to Richard's consternation, Children's Hour was cancelled to make way for an extended news bulletin, invariably in 1941 full of one disaster for the Allies after another.

Emily knew the BBC dressed up its bulletins to make them as palatable as possible; every withdrawal being presented as 'tactical' and British losses allegedly less than those of the enemy. She wanted to believe the radio announcements, but realised in her heart of hearts that the war situation seemed to be deteriorating rapidly.

***

Chapter 12

Who Dares?

Emily listened avidly to the news broadcasts whenever she could, desperate to discover the course of events in the world outside the village of Pecket Well. 1941 proved to be the low point in the war for the British, despite propaganda attempts to make it seem otherwise. The fall of France had made people sceptical about the half-truths and lies to which they were subjected. As Churchill once said: '*In wartime, truth is so precious that she should always be attended by a bodyguard of lies.*'

One of the heaviest raids on London occurred on the 10th May 1941 when over three thousand people were killed. Conditions in Britain at this time were grim indeed; the armed forces needed more men, but so did the munitions industry.

A few weeks after the May 1941 air raid, Walter telephoned Emily one morning from London: 'The bank has released me and I'm volunteering to join the army. This may be the last you hear from me for some time, particularly if I'm posted overseas. If you could see what they've done to London, you'd understand.'

The call distressed Emily terribly; she really might lose him and be stranded with Richard in a tiny village where she had no real friends. She burst into tears, utterly devastated and unable to speak. How could he leave her like this?

Walter attempted to explain: 'I tried to join the intelligence service rather than face call up into the infantry. I can read

German and understand it when spoken, but my accent leaves much to be desired. The interview panel rejected me for that role but expressed interest in my CV and recommended me for an officer training course. I've no idea where I might end up.'

Emily felt abandoned and depressed. Her life had gone full circle; she found herself alone with her precious son, dumped in a place only eleven miles from her parents in Halifax. Had her elopement all been in vain? She reflected: 'I used to pride myself on having achieved all my objectives in life but look at me now. I did marry my Jimmy but now he won't listen to me and we're separated. I did escape from Halifax and my dominating father but now I live in a hovel only a few miles away from him. James is just as masterful, fancy parking me here in this village with no proper facilities to have a bath. I do have my Richard but that is not enough.'

After school that afternoon, Emily took her son to her special place near Hardcastle Crags where Walter had proposed to her. Whilst the little boy hunted for rabbit holes, she wept quietly to herself. Her loss felt even more palpable here; all she could do was to pray silently that one day her Jimmy would be returned to her.

It began to rain gently and she felt as if heaven was shedding tears in sympathy with her distress. She felt wretched yet the experience gave her the strength and determination to struggle on; she must not let her husband down when he volunteered to serve his country.

***

Some weeks after the traumatic telephone call, James paid Emily a surprise early morning visit at her cottage. He had received a telephone call from Walter the previous evening, the first contact with his son for over two months. She went pale at the thought that something terrible might have happened to her Jimmy.

But James had some good news: 'Walter is about to start a week's leave which he has been ordered to spend in the Isle of

Man. He wants you and Richard to take the Saturday morning ferry from Liverpool to Douglas and join him. I promised to give you the message but my advice is not to go and certainly not to take Richard. Liverpool is a prime target for German bombers; the docks have suffered heavy bombing seven nights in a row and the whole area is a disaster zone.'

Even though the raids had all been at night, dare she risk such a dangerous journey, if indeed it proved possible for civilians to travel to the Isle of Man?

James had been confident that Emily would take his advice but she exclaimed defiantly: 'We're going. If he wants us there, that's it. I love him and it may be the last time I ever see him alive.' She quickly packed a few clothes and bundled her son into James' car. They would go to Hebden Bridge immediately and see if trains were running to Manchester and from there to Liverpool.

The journey to the port proved surprisingly easy; for once Manchester Victoria Station and the railways seemed to be functioning normally, well as near to normal as they ever did in wartime. Yet on arrival at the docks around 12 noon, they found everything in chaos caused by a heavy air raid during the previous night, fire engines and police were everywhere.

Which jetty did the ferry depart from; had it survived the air-raid? The signs to the booking office directed them to a bombsite still smouldering from the previous night's raid. People seemed too traumatised to help - but the location of the ferry office could hardly be a state secret - could it?

In desperation, she sought out the police station and explained the situation to the desk sergeant. Did she have a pass? No. If her husband was in the army, did she have a letter or telegram from him? No. Then a flash of inspiration occurred to her: 'My husband will have all the necessary papers. He'll be waiting for us by the ferry, but I can't find the ferry.'

This seemed to solve the sergeant's dilemma. 'Trouble is there may not be a ferry today. There are warnings of severe gales; they won't risk sailing if there's a severe storm.'

Tears welled in Emily's eyes; there must be a ferry and they needed to be on it. The sergeant gave her directions to the pier where the ferry normally docked and they hastened there as fast as they could. And there she lay, a real old bucket of a ferry dating from the days of the Titanic and rather the worse for wear.

Yet she found no sign of Walter; no message from him; no papers. A member of the crew chose to be helpful: 'Are you sure you really want to sail in the teeth of a gale to the prison island? It's no holiday resort these days you know.'

Emily did not know anything about the Isle of Man, but chose to keep that to herself. 'My husband is in the army. He's sent for us and I must see him.'

The crew allowed them on board, but Emily could see from the expression on their faces that they were looking at her in disbelief. Could this respectable mother really want to take her young son on such a journey? The Captain told her: 'We won't be sailing until the wind abates, but we will be the first ferry to leave.' No one said anything about being the first to arrive.

***

Half an hour later, the Captain announced: 'I intend to sail now, rather than risk remaining in the port after dark when the bombing starts. It will be a rough trip and if anyone wants to get off, they are welcome to do so.'

Emily shook her head: 'We are going - no argument about that'. She and Richard stood by the rail on the bow of the ferry watching the sailors cast off - and they were away. Her mood brightened perceptibly, they really were going after all.

She clearly remembered sailing eight years earlier from Liverpool to Boston in the Cunard liner on her honeymoon. The memories came flooding back as she showed Richard the familiar landmarks when they came into view: 'Look, there's the historic Albert Dock; it seems to have been requisitioned by the Navy. And over there's the Cunard Building, and look the Three

Graces and there's the huge pier at which the liners berthed. That's the pier from which your dad and I left for America.'

Several of the buildings were destroyed or severely damaged, but the landmarks remained recognisable. The battered old ferry bore no resemblance to the luxurious liner but in her imagination she relived going on her honeymoon, one of the great events of her life.

As they approached the open sea, one of the sailors handed out life jackets. 'Captain's orders ma'am. All passengers must wear life jackets; it's going to be rough out there. And keep the lad well away from the edge; we don't want him swept overboard.'

The ferry cleared the estuary and caught the full force of the wind; lumps of charred wreckage floated by; this would be no pleasure trip. A damaged destroyer limped towards them on its way to the dockyard, but there could be no turning back - or could there?

The loudspeaker boomed out: 'This is the Captain. If the weather deteriorates much further, we will have to put back into Liverpool.' Emily felt horrified and prayed desperately that the ferry would continue its voyage. It began to roll with the swell; not just forwards and backwards but side to side - up and down, up and down, side to side.

Richard vomited, retching again and again. Emily, grateful not to feel sick herself, comforted her son though with mixed feelings of sympathy, astonishment and disgust. 'Let's just sit on those sacks over there under the bridge and you'll feel better.'

A sailor rushed over and shouted angrily: 'Stop that child! He can't be sick over those sacks; they're full of rabbits. Someone's got to eat those rabbits.'

Emily told him: 'No power on earth can stop Richard from throwing up.' The sea intervened by breaking right over the bow and drenching them all, washing away all traces of the crime. The sailor laughed: 'Never mind. We'll feed the rabbits to the bloody Germans. Hold tight to the stair rail and you'll be OK.'

They both grabbed the rail; nothing on earth could have induced Emily to sit on a sack of dead rabbits, with or without the distinctive flavour so recently added by her son. The ferry ploughed on, making headway against the wind painfully slowly. The gale increased in intensity and the waves began to wash over the deck. The crew put up storm shutters to help keep the water out, but this meant no one could see the waves or lean over the rail to be sick.

The deck suddenly filled with very sick people doing their best to avoid one another but not always succeeding. They were shut in and experienced a feeling of claustrophobia, of sheer wretchedness - and the stench. 'Surely matters can get no worse?' Emily thought. But just then, the ferry gave a violent lurch to starboard and came close to capsizing.

The loudspeaker came on again: 'This is the Captain. Hold on tightly; do not panic.' The ferry suddenly lurched to port, staggering under the blow of another huge wave, but righting itself. 'Sorry about that. We've sighted a periscope looking at us a mile to port. I've reported it but the Royal navy has no submarine in the area. We have to assume it's a U-Boat. My orders are to proceed at full speed ahead and to steer in random zigzags. In this storm, we will from time to time be broadside on to the waves. May God be with us all.'

For the first time, Emily herself was sick, very sick. She thought: 'What have I done bringing my precious son into such danger against everyone's advice?' Now, they could only sit there on the deck, holding on to the stair rail like grim death and pray for deliverance.

Emily never learned whether the U-Boat fired torpedoes at the ferry. If it did, in the tremendous rise and fall of the swell they might easily have passed underneath the hull. Then again, the ferry and its passengers were hardly the biggest fish in the sea.

***

Emily and Richard arrived in Douglas, thankful to be still alive but sick and very unsteady on their feet. Walter looked very grave at their shattered appearance as he rushed forward to greet them, but he too bore little resemblance to the bank official who waved them goodbye in Bournemouth all those long months ago. He wore an officer's uniform, complete with revolver in a holster, and looked very fit - at least two stones lighter than before.

Despite her nausea and fatigue, Emily threw herself into his arms and smothered him with kisses; determined to make the best of her time with her husband. This really would be a second honeymoon for her; Walter beamed as soon as he realised that both of them were unscathed by their ordeal.

He ushered them away from the ferry terminal onto a nearly deserted promenade lashed by wind, rain and spray from the sea. 'I've booked us into the Sefton hotel,' he explained. 'It's only ten minutes' walk away and nearly empty. There are virtually no holidaymakers; just a few military people and businessmen.'

They heard the tramp of marching feet approaching. 'Get that child out of the way, sir,' a sergeant yelled. A column of perhaps a hundred men in grey German uniforms marched sloppily down the centre of the road towards them, escorted by a British corporal in front, a sergeant in the rear and four soldiers on each side. The allied soldiers made no attempt to march but brandished the bayonets on their rifles threateningly at the column. The NCOs both held tommy guns across their chests in the manner of experienced men who knew how to use them and hated Germans.

Emily gazed at the column at first in amazement, then horror. She remarked quietly to her husband: 'We are in danger here; there aren't enough guards. If the prisoners make a break for it, scores of them will get away, even though those two do look as if they want to use their submachine guns. We simply aren't safe standing here; they might snatch Richard.'

'Don't worry,' Walter assured her. 'I have my revolver and I've been trained how to use it. None of those men are Nazis; the Hitler youth aren't allowed out of the camps. Anyhow, we have crack troops no more than five minutes' drive away; Commandos training for an operation and then there's my lot.' He would not elaborate about who his lot were and Emily winced at the implication. This certainly was not a holiday destination any more.

The Sefton, a four-star Victorian luxury hotel with high ceilings and large rooms far superior to the Bournemouth hotel where they were last together, seemed to defy the odds. A porter showed them to a spacious double bedroom with a sea view and an en-suite bathroom. Walter gave him a tip then ordered Richard: 'Go and take a bath, then you can play with this toy wooden warship which I've bought for you. I'll tell you when it's time to get ready for tea.'

His parents tearfully hugged one another and then made love with a passion brewed during long months of separation. Then they made love again and Emily felt uplifted, even happier than at any time on their first honeymoon. She thought: 'What a relief, my husband still loves me every bit as passionately as I love him. His insistence on volunteering for the army had made me worry about his fidelity but now I know that my doubts were groundless. I must be more trusting in future.'

Over breakfast the next morning in the ornate dining room, Walter explained that he had just successfully completed a gruelling officer's training course: 'One of the guys there served as a regular staff sergeant, fresh from fighting in the desert and being commissioned in the field. The instructors gave him hell but now his commission has been confirmed he'll always be an officer. I helped him through some of the more technical stuff; he gave me a hand on the rifle range by putting three bullseyes into my target. He explained that he wanted to avoid becoming a sniper and needed a few weak scores. They've stopped making blank cartridges; the machine guns firing low over our heads used live ammunition; that really does make you keep your head down.'

Emily winced at the thought of the machine gun. 'Did you suffer any casualties?' she enquired but Walter grinned and shook his head. 'The army are evaluating the results of the course and I don't know where I'll be posted at the end of my leave. When I do, it'll be secret and I won't be allowed to tell you.' She expressed her disappointment but recognised that such secrecy had become a necessary fact of life.

The week passed all too quickly; on wet days they stayed in the hotel and Walter showed Richard how to make model warships out of balsa wood with pins for guns. At night, Emily and Walter made breathless love with a passion made all the greater by the realisation that they might never see one another again.

One evening over dinner, he told her something of the horrors of his life in London during the Blitz: 'I remember vividly walking passed St. Paul's Cathedral to find Ludgate Hill one mass of flames engulfing the whole of the buildings on the south side, every window alight from end to end, with flames towering high above them into the sky. Firemen were spraying water on the walls opposite but the bricks were so hot it turned to steam.

'Like thousands of others, I spent most nights in an underground station, relatively safe but thoroughly uncomfortable. The Government closed the branch line to the Aldwych and converted the tunnels into an air-raid shelter, much better to be there rather than constantly being disturbed by trains.

'I hated the sight of familiar buildings hiding behind sandbags, the skyline sprouting barrage balloons and the searchlights seeking out targets for the anti-aircraft guns. I found the smell of burning buildings and bodies and the growing number of bomb sites unbearable. You have no idea how much damage is being inflicted daily on the city.

'Then just after Christmas, the Germans dropped thousands of incendiary devices on the City area of London creating a fire storm which raged out of control for days. This devastated the area close to St Paul's Cathedral and permanently changed the landscape; but somehow the Cathedral itself still survives.

'Are you surprised that all the death and destruction which I saw with my own eyes and the stench of rotting bodies, some of which I had to move myself, made me need to fight back?'

***

Eventually, the weather improved and they all spent a little time on the beach; Emily kept tight hold of Walter's hand as they watched little Richard playing in the sand. She had no interest in exploring the sights, preferring to return to their hotel as soon as her son showed any sign of becoming bored with his sand castle.

At the end of the week, the time came for her to go back to Pecket Well. Miserable Emily held on to her husband for as long as she could but in the end they parted with tears in their eyes.

The sun shone and the ferry ran to time in a calm sea. She told herself: 'Life must go on; we are fortunate enough still to be alive in this terrible war. It's no good my feeling depressed. My Jimmy still loves me and I will look after Richard as best I can and devote all my efforts helping to educate him. We won't be hungry, I will work on the farm like a Land Girl.'

***

Chapter 13

A Changing World

24th June 1941

The German invasion of Russia without warning on 22nd June 1941 came as a shock to Stalin, but a great relief to the British population. As an immediate consequence of this attack, German bombing of Britain miraculously ceased for some months and switched to the Eastern front.

On her return journey from the Isle of Man, Emily noticed a significant change to the docks in Liverpool; no bombs had fallen on the port over the previous forty eight hours and dock workers no longer seemed so crushed and dazed. The port hummed with activity; men bustled about unloading cargo from a newly-arrived Atlantic convoy onto fleets of army lorries.

The Captain announced: 'Our arrival in the port is being delayed so that a flotilla of escort destroyers can leave harbour to meet another convoy.' Emily watched them steaming out at speed in line ahead, a magnificent sight which filled their hearts with hope and caused her and the other passengers to wave and cheer.

However, the second half of 1941 continued to be disastrous for Britain; the Allies lost control of the Mediterranean enabling the Germans to reinforce Rommel in the desert and the large British garrison in Singapore surrendered in February 1942. Emily sobbed at the news.

Meanwhile, on 7th December 1941, the Japanese attacked Pearl Harbour, crippling the American Pacific fleet and bringing America into the war. Emily, like most of the British population, hoped that the power of America would lead the Allies to ultimate victory as it had done in the First World War. British concern centred on the Atlantic and the need to protect the vital supply convoys.

From the moment she returned to Pecket Well from the Isle of Man, Emily became a compulsive follower of the BBC news, as did all with relatives away in the forces. She listened with incredulity to Churchill's inspiring broadcast to the Nation:

'I see the ten thousand villages of Russia where the means of existence is wrung so hardly from the soil - - I see advancing upon all this in hideous onslaught the Nazi war machine, with its clanking, heel-clicking, dandified Prussian officers, its crafty expert agents fresh from the cowing and tying down of a dozen countries. I see also, the dull, drilled, docile, brutish masses of the Hun soldiery plodding on like a swarm of crawling locusts.'

She tried to work out where the army might send her husband and how the Allies were faring on that front. It turned out to be a futile exercise; all her guesses were wrong, but somehow it made her feel closer to him. She worried and dreaded that he might be posted to Russia.

In May 1942, the reinforced German Afrika Korps attacked in North Africa; Panzer divisions swept into the desert; Allied forces withdrew in disorder and were driven back to El Alamein, only forty miles from Alexandria.

As she listened in horror to Winston Churchill's speech about the fall of Tobruk, Emily formed the view that Walter would most likely be posted to fight in the desert. She started to tremble and tears came into her eyes as she heard on the wireless Churchill announce:

'- - We have lost upwards of fifty thousand men, - - - a great mass of material, and, in spite of carefully organised demolitions, large quantities of stores have fallen into enemy hands. Rommel has advanced nearly four hundred miles through the desert - - - We

are at this moment in the presence of a recession of our hopes and prospects in the Middle East and in the Mediterranean unequalled since the fall of France.'

Just what would she do if her Jimmy never came back? She told herself: 'None of the men in the village interest me in the slightest and I cannot afford to return to Petts Wood, even if it eventually becomes safe. Hebden Bridge, perhaps, but that would be little better than Halifax. I'll just have to let events take their course.'

***

The senior mistress at the village school called Emily in and explained: 'Your son can now read and write fluently and is at the stage where he would normally be moved into the senior class. However, he is two years younger than all the other pupils in that class and I'm concerned that he'll be bullied when he outshines them. You come from Halifax and worked at the building society; your son needs to be prepared to go to the grammar school and we don't have the resources to do that here.'

Emily remained adamant that she would never return to Halifax, but agonised about the potential damage her decision would do to her son. She desperately needed to discuss the matter with her husband, but how could she get in touch with him?

James realised that Walter joining the army had made her depressed and tried to reassure her by increasing his visits to the cottage and making sure that she had enough money. She tried hard not to cry at the news of defeats and atrocities and gained much comfort from prayer; a gift learned from her father!

***

Allied reinforcements began to pour into the desert; but only in October 1942, did the Allied counterattack commence; the defeat of Rommel at El Alamein developed into the first important allied victory of the war. Now, at last, after three years of war, the Panzers were stopped. At home in Britain, people joyously celebrated this news and hope of victory returned for Emily.

Hitler ordered his battle cruisers then stationed in Brest to force their way through the English Channel and prevent supplies reaching Russia. Unfortunately, the British fleet in its weakened state found itself outgunned. The heavy batteries at Dover opened up but missed their target; six torpedo carrying fleet air arm Swordfish attacked the Germans, but all were shot down.

This incident, witnessed by many living on the south coast, could not be kept secret and made a considerable impact on Emily and the public's morale. Everyone knew about censorship of the press; were the Royal Navy's losses such that it no longer controlled the Channel? What would happen if the Germans assembled another invasion fleet?

Emily felt that things should be improving; Britain no longer fought alone against overwhelming odds. The enormous armies of Russia and the United States of America were both on its side, yet everywhere the Allies were in full retreat. The German blitzkrieg against Russia slowed but by no means halted; the Japanese still advanced and now threatened both India and Australia / New Zealand.

The BBC News carried updates on the heroic defence of Stalingrad, Leningrad and other Russian cities. Emily like others drew strength from this; perhaps the Nazi war machine could be stopped after all? Night time raids on Britain began again in April 1942; the British public needed to know that they were not alone in suffering from German bombs.

***

One evening, the growl of a mass of low-flying aircraft, perhaps thirty or so German bombers overhead, disturbed Emily and Richard at home in their cottage. He identified them from the card given to him at school; there could be no doubt about it but what were they doing flying over Pecket's hills? They watched intrigued, but not really alarmed; bombers occasionally flew nearby on their way to targets in Leeds or Huddersfield, but many weeks had passed since they last did so.

Suddenly, the sky lit up; the bombers circled and started dropping flares but surely sheep and heather would be all they could see? Then Emily remembered that Pecket mill manufactured, so she believed, secret war work. She firmly bolted the door and made her son lie under the bed. Were they going to have an air raid? Having thoroughly frightened her, the planes flew on and she spent a restless night worrying about whether they might return.

The following afternoon to her astonishment, Walter arrived unannounced in an army jeep driven by an attractive blond sergeant in her twenties. This was the first time she had seen or heard from her husband since visiting him in the Isle of Man. Emily and Richard were having tea; the boy jumped up from the table, spilling the milk in his excitement, and rushed over to hug his father with shouts of: 'Daddy, daddy'.

Walter wore battle dress and Emily noticed that the revolver in a holster was tied to his wrist by a lanyard. 'Don't you touch that gun,' he warned his son as he gave him a quick hug and Emily a peck on the cheek. 'It's loaded. I'm not on leave; I'm here on army business. My sergeant is out in the lane looking for any sign of suspicious activity in the village.'

He questioned them about what they had seen the previous evening. 'So it's true, Emily; we suspected that it might be a silly rumour. The Home Guard will have to cope initially, but we'll reinforce them when we know what we're up against.'

Emily frowned: 'You can hardly regard the local Home Guard here as a serious force, even if it does have a certain amount of ingenuity. Its principal weapon consists of twenty or so heavy circular concrete blocks deposited in a line just below the crest of the hill high above the main road to Hebden Bridge. If enemy vehicles attempt to use the road, the idea is to roll the blocks down on top of them and crush whatever gets in the way.'

Walter exploded: 'Idiots; we're worried about enemy paratroops landing on the moors where there is absolutely nothing to stop them and these people think they're playing some kind of glorified marbles. If the Germans come, Emily, you must put the oak dining table on its side against the bed and hide underneath. Here's a telephone number where you can contact me if anything happens.'

He handed her a slip of paper, gave her another quick peck on the cheek and rushed out of the door before she could talk to him about Richard's education. She followed him out of the cottage to wave goodbye and discovered that the attractive sergeant sitting in the driving seat of the jeep greeted him not with a smart salute but a cheery smile.

This totally unexpected visit shattered Emily; not only did she have to bear the prospect of German paratroopers dropping in force on the moors nearby which destroyed any illusion about the cottage being safe; but her husband never gave her a proper cuddle. They always hugged; his failure to do so distressed her and why did he call her Emily instead of Betty?

Could it be that he had found a new younger more attractive lady friend, that girl sergeant certainly looked gorgeous? Everyone talked about wartime romances, but surely her Jimmy wouldn't betray her, would he? Suppose he only met her rival after being posted to Manchester; she guessed he came from there because she recognised the contact telephone number which he had given her as a Manchester number.

She did not have much sleep for the next few nights; other thoughts kept creeping into her mind. Walter's manner seemed to have fundamentally changed and she did not like it. Indeed she realised with a shock that she now thought of him as 'Walter' rather than as 'her Jimmy'.

He used to ask people to do things for him and say 'please'; now she heard from the villagers that he shouted orders and expected to be obeyed. His abrupt departure made her suspect there would be no discussion of tactics with the Home Guard, it would be told: 'you are a shambles' and ordered what to do.

Then again, why did he not let her know about being based so near Pecket and save her worrying about the war in the desert?

Walter's visit impressed the villagers; an officer and his family living in our village; imagine. It made a very different impression on Emily; if he started ordering her about, she could never tolerate that and life would become very difficult for both of them.

She thought: 'I do love my Jimmy but I'm in danger of losing him either to that blond sergeant or to the army, which is changing him from being the kind decent man that I married into an efficient fighting machine. I must do something about it urgently but what?'

The previous winter in the cold damp cottage ranked as the most miserable experience she had ever suffered. Bombing of British cities seemed to have become sporadic; she needed to be near her husband, now apparently based in Manchester; Richard needed a better school. She decided to move to Manchester as soon as possible, whilst they still could once more be together, but she worried how Walter would react. It took her a few days to pluck up the courage to ring the contact number and find out.

***

Chapter 14

Manchester

Would it really be sensible to move from a quiet village to a prime target in the middle of an all-out war? Emily remembered all too well her horror at seeing the burning ruins around Manchester Victoria Station when she first arrived in the city as an evacuee. Since then it had suffered a further heavy night raid in June 1941 and numerous other lesser raids subsequently. James, who visited the city on business regularly, assured her that daytime raids were a thing of the past and night raids now concentrated on industrial rather than residential areas.

Walter's talk of enemy paratroops landing on the moors had thoroughly alarmed her, but what would happen if she moved to Manchester and then the army posted her husband overseas as seemed likely? Would his military duties permit her to see him? She loved him deeply, but he seemed so business-like and unromantic on his last visit that she needed to be with him again to reassure herself that their relationship remained intact.

She telephoned him from the Post Office one afternoon after it closed, full of indecision. He told her: 'The best way to get through this war is to live one day at a time; no one can foresee the future. You know my philosophy of predestination - that if a bomb has your name on it, you are dead whatever you do; and if not, it will miss you. This belief made my life in the London blitz bearable.

'Please do come and join me here in Manchester. It shouldn't be too difficult to find somewhere for you to live, much better than that cottage for next winter, and Richard needs a decent school. I've only recently been posted here and visited you in Pecket on the first opportunity I could. Sorry not to have been able to spend more time with you and seeming to be a bit abrupt. Your description of the Home Guard made me realise that we really will have a military emergency on our hands if enemy paratroops attack.

'I'll find a school for Richard, but I may be sent away at very short notice. I know of a ground floor flat in Victoria Park which would be just right for the two of you. Before the war, this used to be one of the more pleasant residential areas in Manchester, but a bomb destroyed one of the grand houses and people moved away. The flat is in a small block finished just before the war and never fully occupied. No Anderson shelter, but that surely is a plus point as far as we are concerned!'

Although he seemed quite commanding about where she must live, Emily allowed herself to be persuaded; any time spent with him would be a bonus, the Isle of Man taught her that. Perhaps next time they were together she might become pregnant?

The flats, designed as first homes for single people or young couples, each contained a good-sized living room with an alcove, a small bedroom just large enough for a double bed, a reasonable kitchen and a tiny bathroom. Walter rented two flats back to back and the landlord, grateful at having at last found a tenant in such a war stricken area, allowed him to install an inter-connecting door.

James drove Emily and Richard over to the flat in his car one sunny day at the end of August. To her horror, she found that the walls were painted light grey and that linoleum covered the concrete floor; no skirting boards or coving and only one light in each room. She resolved to buy two second-hand standard lamps as soon as possible and James promised to arrange transport for their meagre furniture from the cottage, minus the tin bath.

At least she would now be able to have a proper bath and

use an inside toilet; that would be a big improvement to her standard of living. Richard asked: 'Can I use one of the baths to float the model boats which dad showed me how to make? Emily patted him on the head and gave him a kiss, relieved that he seemed to be happy to live in Manchester and face the challenge of a new school.

Blackout curtains covered the windows and when drawn gave much needed privacy from passers-by in the busy road outside. She would not have chosen such a flat herself but at least the rent would be cheap and affordable. She decided to do her very best to make it a liveable home and to conceal her distaste for it from her Jimmy; he seemed beset with enough problems without her adding to them.

At this time, Walter's army life allowed him to have the occasional day's leave; his quarters were within easy reach of the flat. The absence of parachute landings and bombs allowed the army to permit this provided he stayed in the city. Manchester's considerable strategic significance made it necessary to keep troops in the area able and ready to defend it.

He used these precious days of liberty to help Emily settle into the flat. Thrilled at being together again with her Jimmy, she initiated love-making at every opportunity. His enthusiastic response soon assuaged her fear that she might have a rival; actions were so much more pleasurable and persuasive than verbal assurances. She quickly dismissed her worries on that score and felt ashamed at having doubted her husband. Walter visited her whenever he could and each time they made passionate love as if this would be their last time together before he received orders posting him abroad.

She transferred her own war work to a sub-post office easily accessible from her flat. Any Saturday when Walter enjoyed some leave, they visited the suburb of Wythenshawe with its park which contained a vast expanse of grass surrounded by rhododendron bushes. She wondered why the grassland survived without being ploughed up and planted with vegetables as part of the 'Dig for Victory' campaign.

She missed the regular supplement to their rations provided by the farmer in return for a helping hand, but everyone else seemed to cope with rationing and so would she. As an officer's wife, she refused to supplement her diet by buying food on the black market.

***

Richard became something of a worry as like many wartime children he needed to cope for himself from an early age. Child minders, other than friends and relatives, were a rare luxury and Emily never found one in Manchester who would help her. Fortunately, her son made friends with another boy from the same school who lived nearby. They roamed the bomb damaged ruins in Victoria Park together, under strict orders not to venture further afield and not to touch any war debris left lying around.

Emily smiled to herself when she saw how quickly her son seemed to be growing up. Toy town stories became a thing of the past, replaced by a new BBC program broadcast immediately before the six o'clock news. He now followed the adventures of 'Dick Barton Special Agent' who could be relied upon to start every fifteen minute episode by escaping from impossible odds only to end in even greater danger. Of course, he always contrived to be a survivor and, in a world of censorship, that needed to be the perceived destiny of the Nation.

Walter obtained a place for the boy at the preparatory school for William Hulme's Grammar School. It had never evacuated but remained at its original site throughout the war. Now, Richard had to learn to cope with homework and strict school discipline.

Emily took her son to school for the first week of term and showed him where to change busses. From then on he would have to cope by himself and travel to and from school alone, furnished with a gas mask, notwithstanding his tender age. She did not like this, but managed to arrange that most days his friend travelled with him.

Emily grew to like Manchester. People generally helped one another showing a great patriotic spirit; they were all in it together against the Germans. Crime existed but to a far lesser extent than before the war, particularly a black market to mollify rationing. Muggers faced too many citizens with military training who carried guns and knew how to use them.

Sadly, the cessation of bombing proved to be only temporary. The Luftwaffe once again started heavy night time bombing of British cities; but by now the Americans were here and the Allies could and did retaliate.

In one particular raid on Manchester, a year or so after Emily moved there, the bombing occurred some distance away from her flat. As always, the censored news which she heard on the radio downplayed its severity. She decided that Richard should go to school as usual; took him to the stop for the first bus to see if it ran, and when it came waved him goodbye.

Later on, he told his mother what happened: 'When I got off the bus which you put me on, I found a long queue for the second bus. People seemed surprised to see me; the nurse standing in front of me in the queue asked if I didn't know there'd been an air raid. Others said you'd have gone to work and I'd better go on to school.

'When a bus came; its top deck had been smashed in by a bomb but the lower deck was still OK apart from cracked windows. "Come on," the lady conductor shouted. "We'll take as many of you as can cram on board. Nobody upstairs, it's not safe. To hell with the regulations about how many passengers we can carry; this is war.'

Emily felt guilty at having sent her son to school in such circumstances but proud at the way he coped with the situation.

The school made its pupils' education as normal as possible; they did a fantastic job and the boys all tried their hardest. Emily knew that Richard and his friends were acutely aware of the war and followed the news programs attentively; his father in the army and bombing made the conflict personal for him. The children drew particular comfort from reports about the heroic resistance shown by the Russians defending Leningrad and Stalingrad; Britain no longer stood alone in its struggle for survival.

***

As the months passed, the war situation began to improve and news bulletins became in general more optimistic. In particular, Britain no longer lived under the horrendous threat of invasion; American forces were arriving in even greater numbers and making their presence felt particularly in the south of England. Bombing raids on Britain tailed off; the Royal Air Force at last commanded the skies over the United Kingdom.

The Allies drove the German army out of North Africa and succeeded in capturing Southern Italy. The Russians began their unstoppable advance and the Royal Navy sank the last German battleship. The Allied invasion of Northern France could not be far away but life at home in Britain remained a struggle for Emily like everyone else.

Rationing became more severe than ever as new improved U-boats, one of Hitler's much vaunted secret weapons, attacked supply routes and disrupted the struggle to bring food and war materials across the Atlantic. There were shortages of nearly everything, rationed or not. The winter blackout induced a misery of its own. Clothes were now rationed; good quality clothes surprisingly took no more coupons than their cheaper equivalents.

One sunny day in the late spring of 1944, sitting under a rhododendron bush in Wythenshawe Park, Walter broke the news: 'This must be our last visit here. I will no longer be able to spend my leave with you; the army require me full time and could be about to post me away from Manchester.'

He took her back to the flat where they said a long and passionate farewell when the time came for him to leave. 'Please write to me whenever you can,' Emily sobbed. 'I promise to write to you every day without fail. I love you, I always will for the rest of my life, I really do.'

Walter shook his head sadly. He looked grave: 'All mail will be censored for security reasons. I will always love you, you know that, but no correspondence will be allowed so please don't write.' He gave her a big hug and kiss and tore himself away with tears in his eyes before she could say any more.

***

Chapter 15

Separation

It became obvious that the Allies were about to launch an initiative, but information about when and where in France the attack would take place remained a closely guarded secret from the civilian population and from the Germans. Emily worried about her Jimmy: 'Where is he? If he's still in Manchester, surely he'll let me know? Might he go to France when the Allies land?' The answer to that seemed obvious and it gave her no comfort at all.

She followed the progress of the war in Europe in the newspapers and on the radio and prayed that none of the bullets and shells fired by the Germans bore his name. The Italian campaign did not interest her until just before D-Day, Rome fell and people began to believe that the defeat of Italy could be the beginning of the end of the war.

Her research into news stories about the heroic defence of Stalingrad and Leningrad revived her interest in the war in Russia. Not that she thought Walter might be sent there, but if the Russians could check the invasion of their country and drive the Germans out, perhaps they would take Berlin and destroy Hitler. That would surely shorten the war and save many British lives.

The discovery that the Russian offensive in support of the D-Day landings began soon after D-Day caused her to follow the example of one of her noisy neighbours and sing *The Red Flag* as she went about her housework.

> *'The people's flag is deepest red,*
> *It shrouded oft our martyred dead,*
> *And ere their limbs grew stiff and cold*
> *Their heart's blood dyed its every fold.*
> *Then raise the scarlet standard high,*
> *Within its shade we'll live or die,*
> *Though cowards flinch and traitors sneer,*
> *We'll keep the red flag flying here.'*

She chuckled to herself: 'Walter would not approve of my singing such a political song but he's not here.'

In the following five weeks the Germans were pushed back two hundred and fifty miles out of Russia; the Panzers were not invincible after all.

***

As the days passed and Walter still failed to make contact, Emily became more and more convinced that he must be in Normandy, even if not in the initial landings. At least, she received no telegram about him being killed or missing. She followed developments in the battle for Europe with an increasing sense of horror and foreboding. Would Walter take proper care of himself or would his belief in predestination lead him to volunteer for heroic duties?

What would she do if he died? She thought: 'I don't really know anyone in Manchester who isn't already married. One or two of the customers who come into the Post Office are quite attractive but many of the men are away at the war. Richard's education means that I would need to remain here and struggle on for his sake.'

Any thought of celebrating D-Day which might have gripped the public soon subsided; the landings were heavily opposed and casualties high. Then only a week later, a German rocket attack struck London; no aircraft this time, just huge missiles armed with one ton of high explosive. Hitler called this new secret terror weapon the V1, the first in a new series of terror weapons with which he planned to smash Britain's will to continue the fight.

Over three thousand V1 rockets were launched against Britain in the next five weeks, killing or maiming over two thousand people and destroying or damaging thousands of houses. The bombardment lasted until the middle of September when the launch sites fell to advancing allied troops.

The engines of the V1 made a loud distinctive buzzing sound and stopped when so instructed by a propeller set to measure the distance from the launching site to their target. Whilst the noise continued, people were safe; when it stopped, you knew the bomb had started to fall and you had only seconds to throw yourself flat to avoid the blast. You could tell the direction it travelled, but not how far it would carry before striking the ground in a massive explosion. The rockets flew at all times of day and night whatever the weather, and imposed even more stress on the population than traditional bombing.

A few rockets were aimed at Manchester and some indeed fell on Oldham not far from Emily's flat. Some mothers and children were evacuated from Manchester but Emily decided to remain in her flat. Richard needed to stay at his school and she needed to stay where Walter, the love of her life, could contact her.

The elimination of the V1 threat by advancing troops brought only temporary relief. Hitler followed it up by launching the V2, an even more formidable terror weapon in the form of a rocket with again a one ton warhead. The V2 made no warning engine noise but exploded with an ear-splitting thunderclap and vivid blue flash. When fired, it rose to a height of fifty miles and fell at a speed of four thousand miles an hour. Once launched, nothing could stop it and its victims never knew what hit them. The crater often extended to fifty feet wide and ten feet deep and the force could destroy a whole row of terraced houses.

The real terror of the V2 lay in no one knowing when or where the next one would fall; anyone could die at any time. Emily gritted her teeth and told herself: 'Now is the time to believe that if a V2 has your name on it, you're dead; and if it doesn't, you'll live another day.'

***

December 1944 found the Allies still stuck on the German frontier well short of the Rhine. When Christmas passed and Walter failed to send a card or make contact, Emily began to think she had lost him – if not to the war, to an unknown rival. Other wives received mail from their husbands at the front but she did not.

Separation began to take its toll and she became depressed despite the Allied victories and her usually cheerful approach to life. She spent Christmas in Hebden Bridge with Walter's parents; they too had heard nothing from him, but even the family gathering and the presents they lavished on Richard failed to bring a smile to her face. Their attic remained as cold as ever and James just as overpowering; it came as a relief to return to her flat in Manchester with its happy memories of time spent with her Jimmy.

***

As British and American armies crossed the Rhine, the Red Army overcame fierce German counterattacks launched against it; encircled various strong points and reached the river Oder, a mere thirty five miles from Berlin. General Eisenhower, for his part, encircled the Ruhr and drove forward crossing the river Elbe only sixty miles from Berlin.

Stalin began the attack on Berlin with massed forces along a two hundred mile front and by the 25th April surrounded it and met up with elements of the US First Army. The main allied forces halted on the banks of the rivers Elbe and Mulde - Russians to the East; Americans and British to the West. In Berlin, Hitler shot himself quickly followed by the suicide of Goebbels and Himmler. Germany finally surrendered unconditionally on 9th May 1945 to Emily's huge relief. Would she at last be reunited with her Jimmy?

The day Germany surrendered, virtually the entire British population began two days of wild celebrations with impromptu street parties, dancing in the streets and gallons of beer. Not only were they victorious, but somehow they had survived years of bombing and destruction and no longer needed to live in fear of German rocket attacks.

Emily hugged and kissed Walter for a full five minutes when he arrived unannounced at their flat early in the morning of VE Day. 'I apologise for failing to keep in touch, but strict orders were given to me to keep the whereabouts of my unit secret. Information about where the unit was stationed would have assisted the Germans. Please don't ask me about my experiences in the war; they are in the past and I need to forget them and focus on our future for the sake of my health.' His hand began to tremble and Emily squeezed it in hers as she kissed him on the cheek.

***

Churchill made a Victory Broadcast to the Nation: '- *never have the forces of two nations fought side by side and intermingled in the lines of battle with so much unity, comradeship, and brotherhood, as in the great Anglo-American Armies.*' He did not include the Russians despite their heroic defence of their cities and subsequent triumphs culminating in the capture of Berlin.

Emily and Walter, like millions of others, regarded the German surrender as the end of the war. He had volunteered to save his country from invasion and destruction; now he wanted to resume his career and enjoy married life. Emily desperately shared this view; she needed her husband to be by her side, not getting killed by the Japanese in some god forsaken jungle on the other side of the world.

However, Churchill's speech signalled further struggle: '- -Forward, unflinching, unswerving, and indomitable till the whole task is done and the whole world is safe and clean.' He probably intended to refer to the Japanese, but could the words include Stalin and the Russians as well?

Emily quickly sensed that the Jimmy in her arms seemed stressed and not at all inclined to take her out to the noisy celebration in the street outside. Most unlike his normal cheery, good humoured self, his breath smelled of whisky even at that early hour and he smoked considerably more than usual.

She pleaded: 'Please tell me what's wrong.'

He replied: 'Now that Hitler's dead, there's a real possibility that once the monsoon rains end, I'll be posted to fight the Japanese in Burma. The Allies are at last advancing over there but progress on that front is woefully slow and may take months.'

That night, Emily could not sleep as Walter tossed and turned struggling with his problems; not just Burma, which he could do nothing about, but how best to resume his career in banking and Richard's future education. His worries about being posted to Burma surprised her and she raised the subject at breakfast the following morning: 'Surely, now that Germany has surrendered the Japanese will soon follow?'

'You don't know them,' he replied. 'They are suicidal fanatics, kamikaze they call it. Churchill wants to restore British prestige by retaking Singapore via Burma and Malaya, but America prefers to seize the Philippines and island hop to Japan. The Japanese still have a powerful fleet including battleships in Singapore. Who can tell what they'll do next?'

***

When the first two days of wild VE Day celebrations were over, Walter intended to devote the rest of his leave to sorting out his career at Lloyds Bank. But the bank declined to discuss his prospects until he received his discharge papers from the army. When he did, Major General Whittaker would decide how best to integrate him back into banking. The General himself had recently been demobbed and put in charge of the bank's personnel department.

Walter's other priority concerned Richard who needed a decent education, preferably at a school which took borders as well as dayboys. They both knew that the bank would move Walter around the country and that would disrupt schooling at a dayboy school.

The London County Council told him about the Gilkes' Dulwich Experiment. Gilkes became Master of Dulwich in 1941 with a remit to rescue it; the school suffered considerable bomb damage and its academic reputation had declined. Sir P.G. Wodehouse attended the College and perhaps his fellow students inspired some of the ebullient, aristocratic characters in his Jeeves and Wooster books.

Walter, smartly dressed in his officers' uniform, went to see the Master to discuss his son's entry and explained that although a Fulbright Scholar, his own career had been interrupted by the war. Gilkes agreed to take Richard provided he passed the College's entrance exam, which in the circumstances could be taken at the preparatory school in Manchester. The eleven plus exam itself had to wait until he started his new school.

***

In the absence of his father, Emily devoted her full attention to Richard and made it her business to follow and support his career at school. Richard did well both academically and on the sports field being made centre forward of his house football team. She watched him play in the inter house competition and congratulated him on his ability as a footballer.

On sports day, Richard only just qualified for the high jump final but as jumping continued, the sun shone and his technique improved. Emily felt proud as his fellow competitors dropped out one by one leaving him the unexpected victor.

At prize giving, the sports mistress caused Richard to sit next to her in the front row rather than with his mother and whispered: 'You'll be making the thank you speech to the headmaster's wife up there who's presenting the prizes.' As she began to tell him what to say, Richard suddenly stood up and apologised: 'I'm sorry Miss but I have to go and collect my high jump prize.' On returning to his seat, the astonished teacher simply said: 'Go and give her these flowers and thank her for coming.'

He returned to the platform and announced: 'Thank you for my prize; now it's my turn to give you your prize.' Everyone enjoyed this, except the sports mistress, and clapped enthusiastically. The applause made Emily so very proud of her young son that a tear trickled down her cheek which she surreptitiously wiped away, hoping no one had seen.

On his last day at preparatory school, leavers (including Richard) were taken by their form mistress to the grammar school itself and shown the class room to which they must report next term. Very different from the lady teachers at the preparatory school, the new master flung open the classroom door and bellowed: 'Stand to attention by the side of your desks when I enter the room and say "good morning sir" when I reach my desk. We expect strict discipline in this school, otherwise you will all be in deep trouble. I will not tolerate slackness.'

When he released them after a lengthy diatribe, the shocked class said goodbye to one another and made their way home. Richard told his mother: 'I am jolly glad I don't have to go back there next term. Dad said he would get me into Dulwich College; the masters there can hardly be so strict or can they?

***

Walter's anxieties about being posted to the far-east turned out to be exaggerated. As the American island hopping approached the Philippines, the Japanese fleet tried to intervene but an American carrier force virtually destroyed it. There remained the Japanese mainland, defended by a well-equipped army of over a million kamikaze fanatical military pledged to fight to the death. All the planning revealed that many thousands of lives would be lost trying to subdue such a well-armed and dedicated enemy.

When the allied leaders met at Potsdam in July 1945 to discuss the future of the world, they learned about the atomic bomb being successfully exploded in New Mexico with awesome results, complete devastation within a one mile radius and massive damage beyond. All were agreed that the bomb must be used and that a net saving of life would result. The first atomic bomb annihilated Hiroshima; the second Nagasaki. Japan agreed to give up the struggle and signed the formal surrender on 2nd September 1945 when Allied fleets sailed into Tokyo Bay.

The war ended at last and the world celebrated, including Emily and Walter who had spent all summer worrying about him being posted to Burma. Now they hugged and kissed and celebrated victory just as joyously as the rest of the population.

But Walter, to their intense frustration, remained in the army. He told his wife: 'With my knowledge of German, I stand a good chance of being posted to the army of occupation in the British Zone of Germany. That would be a complete waste of time. It makes me worry about when I will eventually be demobbed.'

***

Chapter 16

Peace at Last

Walter, with full support and encouragement from Emily, did everything he could to hasten his demobilisation from the army but, despite all his efforts, he remained a low priority. Troops were needed to secure and protect the British zone of newly conquered Germany; to try and prevent Jews from swamping Palestine, and to attempt to preserve the peace whilst India tore itself apart with the creation of Pakistan. Walter wanted no part in such matters but his wishes were irrelevant.

When he eventually received his discharge papers in 1946, he hastened to see Major General Whittaker at Lloyds Bank's head office to discover what position he would be offered. By law, he had the right to be reinstated in his old job as an assistant inspector but he hoped for something materially better.

The General welcomed him back to civilian life: 'I intend to ensure that returning military personnel such as yourself achieve rapid promotion to the seniority which you deserve.'

Walter smiled: 'Thank you very much, sir. My ambition is to become a branch manager; my army experience has taught me how to manage staff efficiently, though I appreciate things are done very differently in civilian life. I hope to move shortly to the London area but would welcome an appointment anywhere that the bank decides to send me.'

The personnel department arranged for him to spend a few weeks on refresher courses and then on the inspection staff, before appointing him assistant manager at Derby branch. The manager introduced his new assistant to customers and generally tutored him on how to perform in his new role. Walter approached the task enthusiastically, free at last to do the work he had always wanted.

Working in Derby meant leaving Emily and Richard behind at a flat which he rented for them in Beckenham, a suburb to the south of London. He promised them: 'This is a purely temporary arrangement; I intend to buy a suitable house in Derby as soon as possible.'

The promotion delighted Walter, but Emily felt disappointed by it. She told him: 'You do realise it means that Richard is inevitably going to become a border at his new school. Nevertheless, I love you dearly and will support you to the best of my ability.'

She thought to herself: 'Walter's experiences in the army and the frustrating delay in being demobbed have changed my Jimmy; he no longer dotes on me in quite the same way, eager to please my every whim. He's always been ambitious, but now he seems to focus on his career in priority to all else. Not only that but he's taken it upon himself to decide where we'll live without listening to my views. Our budget stops us from living anywhere too expensive, but he chose the flat in Beckenham without consulting me and now proposes to buy a house in Derby without even taking me to have look at it.

'I need our marriage to be a partnership; if only he would listen to my views and take them into account, but how can I achieve that? A close loving relationship can only flourish if we live together but that means abandoning my ten year old Richard who needs my support in his new school. Why do I have to choose between father and son; why is life so unfair?'

The self-contained furnished flat in Beckenham, converted from the middle floor of a substantial detached Victorian residence, did not meet her expectations. The fittings in the kitchen and bathroom were of poor quality and a draft penetrated through the windows. The central heating left much to be desired and the absence of any sound proofing meant that she could hear the radio and other noises from the flats above and below; the sparse furnishings were little better. Worst of all, neither she nor Richard knew anyone in Beckenham. All in all, she rated her accommodation in Beckenham far worse than the Manchester flat.

Walter had promised that it would only be a few weeks before he found something better but weeks turned into months. He found a house in Derby but before she could join him, learned of a further promotion to be manager of Keighley branch, a few miles from his family home in Hebden Bridge.

This new promotion fulfilled everything he had hoped for, but the thought of living so near to her family in Halifax appalled Emily. Would she never free herself from living in Yorkshire? But she loved Walter and resolved to stay with him wherever he went; of all her desires that must be the most important once Richard had settled into his new school.

She kept her worries to herself and her mood changed on discovering that property prices in Yorkshire were relatively cheap and that they would be able to purchase a newly built detached house with its own garden. Never before had they been able to buy their own home. She thought: 'All my dreams will come true if only my Jimmy would mellow and listen to my views. How can I make him understand my needs? He's been away from me for too long and become used to making his own decisions.'

**

It fell to Emily to buy Richard's school uniform and introduce him to his new school. The detached semi stiff collars worn with white school shirts proved something of a struggle for her son but Emily helped him to overcome the difficulties of collar studs and tying his tie. Both she and her son found the trauma of his becoming a boarder hard to bear but she hid her tears from him.

Emily worried: 'How will he cope with Dulwich; it's an enormous school; far larger than William Hulme's Grammar School in Manchester? How will he find his way around all by himself at the age of ten?'

She took him to his boarding house, The Orchard, and handed him over to the house master who encouraged her to go rather than have an extended emotional parting. He assured her: 'There are other boys in the house who are the same age as your son and they will all experience their new school together. I suggest Richard, like a number of the others, starts as a weekly boarder, going home after games on Saturday afternoon and returning straight to school on Monday morning.'

***

Peace had returned but ration books still remained a vital part of life. Like all other housewives, Emily faced more severe shopping conditions after the war than during it. Wartime rationing continued contrary to many peoples' expectations and some aspects of it became even harsher. The bacon ration was cut from four to three ounces a week; cooking fat from two to one ounce and soap by an eighth. Emily's ration book only allowed her one egg a week, though Richard's allowed three. Walter took his ration book with him to Derby and Richard's went to boarding school.

For the first time, bread and later potatoes became rationed, allegedly to feed German civilians in the British sector of occupied Germany. In reality, continuous rain in 1946 ruined Britain's wheat crop; the harsh winter of 1946/7 destroyed a massive amount of stored potatoes and a dock strike caused the loss of rotting meat. Moreover, Britain introduced peace time conscription and spent a fortune repairing bomb damage; it lacked the resources to expand food production or the foreign exchange to purchase imports of food.

Bread rationing proved particularly unpopular as only the National Loaf became available. This, made from wholemeal flour with added calcium and vitamins, looked somewhat similar in appearance, but not taste, to today's brown bread. Emily hated it, indeed most people found it grey, mushy and unappetising especially as newly baked bread could not by law be sold until twenty four hours old so that it could be cut into thin slices.

Clothes rationing only ended in May 1949, forcing Emily to use a sewing machine to create outfits which Walter would find attractive. She made every effort to make her natural attributes as glamorous as possible, determined to do her very best to save her marriage.

During the war, the Government had banned ice cream and rationed sugar, sweets, chocolates and confections of all kinds. Years of shortages and restrictions had made people long for the glamour and freedom of peacetime lives. Yet it took years after the end of the war before all rationing ceased, a period of austerity which many people including Emily regarded as utterly unreasonable.

***

Chapter 17

Dulwich College

Whilst Richard boarded at The Orchard, his housemaster required all the boarders, to write a weekly letter home updating their parents on life at Dulwich; insisting that these letters be handed over for posting unsealed so that the contents could be vetted. Emily read and kept every such letter and told her son that she needed to follow his progress.

When Richard first arrived at the boarding house, an older boy quickly introduced him to table tennis and when he tired of that to snooker on a half size table, quite big enough for boys of his age. A few days later, the house captain took Richard on one side and told him:

'You are possibly the youngest boy in the entire school. If anyone tries to bully you, do not bother your parents or the house master but simply tell me. We borders stand together and I will not tolerate bullying and nor will any of the rest of us. I suggest you join the boxing club after school on Tuesdays where you will be taught how to defend yourself.'

Richard did learn how to box and found himself surprisingly good at it. A while later, the gym master announced that he would be selecting the school boxing team for each weight. One boy in particular stood out as best for the lightest weight, but needed to face opposition to qualify.

So it came about that Richard found himself in the ring being worked over by the school champion, who became overconfident and let his guard slip. A good straight left to the head took the boy by surprise, followed by a right uppercut to the chin which saw him sag at the knees and collapse flat on his back on the canvass. In the return match the following week, the champion demonstrated all his skill, much to Richard's discomfort.

A few days later, back in the boarding house boxing gloves were produced and an older boy made Richard box with him, the closest he came to being bullied, except that the two were evenly matched. The housemaster intervened and took the older boy to his study where he drew the curtains and locked the door so that they would not be interrupted.

Richard learned that the master produced a selection of canes of differing lengths and thicknesses and invited his victim to select one. This done the wretched boy bent over the back of a chair and received six strokes of the cane, before being required to shake hands and apologise for his conduct.

Discipline at Dulwich was strict; form masters did not themselves beat boys but sent them to the Headmaster for punishment. However, the prefects regularly handed out canings.

Borders ate lunches separately from day boys and, having surrendered their ration books to the school, 'enjoyed' slightly more nutritious food. Spam and reconstituted potatoes do not rate highly as culinary delicacies with most people. One boy complained to the master in charge that a dead blue bottle lay under his lettuce leaf. 'That's extra meat ration, but you need not eat it. Food is too precious to leave or throw away:' came the unsympathetic reply.

The housemaster himself supervised prep in the evenings, insisting on absolute silence from all boys. The Orchard suffered some war damage, repaired during the summer holidays, but 1946 materials and workmanship left much to be desired. During one prep, a chunk of ceiling fell narrowly missing one of the boarders; would more of it fall? Not surprisingly, the boys found it difficult to concentrate on their homework but were instructed to remain seated at their places in the room and carry on with their studies.

One day, Richard suffered a burst blood vessel in one arm and on being despatched to the school's sanatorium, the nurse in charge told him: 'I've just received a supply of the new wonder drug, penicillin. I'll give you a shot of it just in case the wound becomes infected.' She did and to their joint amazement all signs of the damage healed almost as they watched.

***

Dulwich College, founded by Edward Alleyn in 1619, is a member of the Eton Group and one of Britain's old established famous public schools. Its former pupils include Sir Ernest Shackleton the explorer, Sir P.G. Wodehouse the author, Sir Edward George a Governor of the Bank of England and Brigadier Hunter-Choate whose exploits in the French Foreign Legion and later the SAS are legendary.

In Richard's day there were six Athletic Houses, Marlowe being one, which competed with one another in compulsory sport for all boys on Wednesday and Saturday afternoons. They also competed in singing, drama and a wide range of other activities.

After rugby on the first Wednesday, the Marlowe House Captain, a stocky well-built young man who played as a front row forward for the school's first fifteen, summoned all new boys in his house to a practice session. He explained how to tackle and made them stand in a long line two yards apart. Then, holding a rugby ball in his right hand, he instructed them to try and tackle him while he handed them off with his left.

Their efforts he described as pathetic until he came to Richard, proudly wearing his new black and white shirt, who threw all his weight into a flying tackle. This stopped the marauder in his tracks but did not cause him to fall: 'Quite good, but you must place your head behind me or risk a broken neck,' he instructed the small boy.

Grandfather James insisted on Richard joining the school choir and learning music. This he did with some success, but a success not replicated in the inter-house music competition.

The prefect in charge of the Marlowe house choir decided, at the last moment, that instead of the Elizabethan madrigal which they had struggled all term to master, he would substitute Land of Hope and Glory. The adjudicator and music master were not amused by the hearty rendering of this well-known tune, sung with great gusto by the boys.

Richard's introduction to school life proceeded fairly smoothly, but one morning he loitered in a day dream and only woke from it when the school clock began to strike nine. All boys started the day with assembly, taken by the Master (headmaster) in the Great Hall, which is accessed up an imposing wide staircase. He chose the concrete back stairs in the hope that his disgrace would be less public.

In his haste, halfway up the stairs he tripped bruising his knee. As he picked himself up, the door to the Hall slammed shut with him on the outside, late for assembly and with no excuse. What should he do?

He prayed to God for help and guidance, just as his mother did during the air-raid in Bournemouth. As he prayed, the sun shone through a gap in the clouds and a window directly onto him; he could feel its warmth. Spinning round, he half expected to see God but could not look directly at the sun and the cloud came and covered it again.

Dusting himself down and straightening his tie, he stopped panicking and walked purposefully towards the huge oak door, opening it wide and marching boldly inside. 'Shut the door,' a master hissed at him. 'You can't stay here; you're not in my class. Go and join your own form.'

Richard closed the door with the same loud bang it always made; a bang loud enough to cause the Master to stop his announcement in mid-sentence and the entire school to stare at the commotion. The delinquent walked calmly to the front of the Hall where his class mates were assembled and apologised for being late to the Master.

Silence, total silence; no such thing had ever happened before in the time of Gilkes' headmastership. What would he do? In the event he simply continued: 'Now we are all here, I will start again,' and he repeated his announcement from the beginning. To Richard's surprise, no one rebuked or punished him for being late; if the Master chose to accept his apology that ended the matter.

***

Despite the war, Dulwich maintained many of its pre-war traditions. Boys were addressed by their surnames, never by their first names; masters were called sir as in the military. If a prefect approached, a boy might warn 'KV', a corruption of the Latin *cave* meaning beware.

In 1946, many of the masters, newly demobilised from the forces, struggled to pick up their careers. In particular, Richard's history master had served in the war as a spitfire pilot and in the eyes of the boys could do no wrong. He often reverted to RAF expressions such as *wizard prang* if a boy achieved something difficult.

The geography master had served as a naval officer for much of the war on convoy duty. He told of an incident when his elderly lend-lease US destroyer, equipped with anti-aircraft batteries at each end of the bridge, suffered a dive bomb attack in the western approaches to the English Channel. One of the gunners who opened up on the dive bomber kept on firing as it swept across the ship, causing all the officers on the bridge to throw themselves flat to avoid their heads being shot off. 'Just one of the teething troubles in fighting an unfamiliar vessel!'

Two army physical training sergeants became gym masters and cajoled the boys into learning how to swim, box and keep fit. No swimming costumes were allowed, perhaps partly due to clothes rationing.

One master, in particular, Dulwich inherited from the days of Jeeves and Bertie Wooster; the dreaded Mr Treadgold, a Latin master well remembered by old boys of the era. He used his own personal methods of retaining his pupils' concentration and discipline.

He would call out a boy's surname and order him to construe word for word a section of Latin text. If another boy failed to pay attention, his name would be called to continue. Alternatively, 'Tready' as the boys called him, would select one of the books on his table and hurl it at the offender. Having played cricket for the school's first eleven with some distinction in his youth, he rarely missed.

Then came the time to translate English into Latin; the whole class would write this in their notebooks whilst 'Tready' walked up and down between the desks and subjected any victim not making sufficient effort to a 'bicycle ride'. The teacher would take a tuft of the boy's hair and pull it in a circular motion; the value of teaching Latin at school is to say the least controversial.

***

In the post-war period, all senior boys at Dulwich were required to join the navy, army or air force cadets to prepare them for National Service. This entailed attending school in military uniform on Tuesdays each week and parading and taking military instruction after school. The drill helped to improve discipline and leadership and the instructors were masters with battle experience from the war.

Richard distinguished himself on one map reading exercise which took place on Epsom Downs by following the wrong railway line and becoming hopelessly lost.

The climax to all this training occurred annually when the older cadets took Certificate A, the results of which were passed on to the military authorities. In Richard's year, the examiners comprised a Major, Captain, Lieutenant and Colour Sergeant in the Grenadier Guards who drove into the College through the main entrance in a jeep.

The Sergeant began by marching a squad of boys up and down the quadrangle in front of the clock tower. Unlike the drill they knew, he did not shout left, right, left, right, and halt. Instead, he uttered loud noises which sounded like 'er, or, er, or, aht'. This made the recruits concentrate but led to disaster when he ordered left turn as 'err enn'. Richard, unlike everyone else, turned right, failure loomed.

Next came map reading taken by the Major who produced an Ordinance Survey map and gave two map references; one for allies, the other for enemy. 'Tell me how you would attack', he ordered.

Richard began to indicate where he would position artillery to fire across the valley when the Major interrupted: 'Don't they teach geography at this school; haven't you learned map reading?' It transpired that the close contour lines on the map represented a hill not a valley. What a mistake to make; this looked like failed again!

Weapon stripping and assembly with the Lieutenant passed off smoothly but then came the Captain who tested the boys' efficiency at various crawls. That Richard could do but then came the test question. 'The allies are advancing rapidly. You have just taken a hill only to discover that on the far side there is a steep escarpment with no cover and three enemy machine guns are dug in at the bottom waiting for you. How do you advance?'

Richard had no idea and thanked his lucky stars that he had not fought the war in the Grenadier Guards. The Captain smiled and shook his head: 'You need two squads of nine men each who hold hand grenades with the pin taken out ready to throw in each hand. While you create a diversion to distract the gunners, the first squad rolls down the slope and throws its grenades at the guns. As the machine guns are turned on the first squad the second squad repeats the manoeuvre, immediately followed by your full attack. The point is that the gunners cannot tell who they have hit because bodies and wounded would continue to roll down the slope.'

Richard learned later that suicide attacks of that nature are not encouraged in the British army and that he would be court marshalled if he tried any such thing.

***

Chapter 18

Keighley

Spring 1947

Emily moved into her new three bedroom detached house in Keighley, which had been built with local millstone grit to avoid the national shortage of bricks. She liked the place, despite its being only eleven miles from Halifax, and thought how generous it was of the bank to subsidise Walter's purchase of their home. A pity it had to be kept within the one thousand five hundred square feet floor area limit for new houses imposed by Government regulations but it far surpassed their house in Petts Wood which the Germans had destroyed early in the war.

To celebrate the move, Emily decided to buy herself two new hats and a smart dark red dress. She also visited the hairdresser, one of Walter's valued customers, and opted for a new modern hair style. As a bank manager's wife, she needed to keep up appearances.

When her husband complemented her on the new look, she purred with pleasure and hoped that her Jimmy would really fall for her all over again just like he had done in the old days. She enjoyed mingling with potential customers of the bank at social functions; her time in America made her an attractive and interesting conversationalist.

For Walter, his promotion as manager of the Lloyds Bank branch fulfilled his ambition of becoming a real banker. Once he established himself in his new position and completed the house purchase, all the stress which he had suffered during and immediately after the war fell away.

He joined the local golf club and persuaded Emily to do the same, the members readily welcomed him and his wife. He took lessons in the game from the local professional but, when playing against an important customer, would contrive to lose.

Emily also learned to play golf but particularly enjoyed the social side of the club; she listened entranced to the stories which members told about their experiences in the war. Walter always refused to discuss his own wartime service, claiming that for his own peace of mind he needed and struggled to forget the horrors which he had endured. Emily respected this and felt sorry for him but it sharpened her own curiosity to discover what life had really been like for those involved.

At one of the select golf club dinners, the man sitting next to her, on hearing of her fascination for the subject, told her the story of Maurice Bennet who had joined the Royal Navy Volunteer Reserve at the beginning of the war.

'After surviving escort duties with Malta convoys, Maurice had served on tank landing craft successfully participating in the landings at Salerno in Italy. When ordered back to Britain in order to prepare for D-Day, he volunteered for special duties. Could any such duty be more dangerous than driving a cumbersome landing craft on to a heavily defended beach?

'Maurice commanded a landing craft which had been specially modified to contain one tank and three guns, all with their barrels in fixed positions to fire straight ahead. His orders were to search out a shore battery; aim the guns by steering straight at it, then fire at one thousand yards range.

'D-Day dawned and his and a sister craft went in at full speed ahead, such as their cumbersome crafts could manage, well ahead of the invasion fleet. The beach had been heavily bombed, but it seemed as though they were alone against the might of an invisible German army.

'When a mile out from the shore and still no target identified, suddenly he heard a loud explosion to port. A quick glance revealed that the sister craft had received a direct hit and exploded into pieces. Zigzag. Just in time; another battery closer to Maurice fired at him. This is it; he headed directly for it. Hold on - 1100 yards; wait for it - fire.

'Maurice and the battery fired more or less simultaneously; they missed; he did not. The shell from the tank hit the concrete bunker, but made precious little impression on it. The shells from the three guns exploded - - and produced red smoke.

'Suddenly, a tremendous explosion shook the air; the battery disappeared, not only the battery but the low cliff on which it stood collapsed into the sea. Time to take on the second battery which had sunk their sister craft. Maurice needed to cover half a mile before coming into range; random zigzags and a lot of prayer; they fired several times but he made it. Once again red smoke; once again a huge explosion and half the battery was destroyed.

'He received a signal: "Leave immediate"; no need to be told twice. He turned back out to sea, a sea now covered with scores of landing craft and ships of all types, and as he did so, saw the flash of heavy guns, a Rodney class battleship firing another broadside at the remains of the battery.

'Could there be any survivors from the sister craft? Another signal: "Get out of the bloody way." Dozens of landing craft were powering directly at him on their way to the beach and glory. He made it back - many of the others did not.'

Emily gasped at the bravery of Maurice and his crew, her eyes glowed with excitement as the story unfolded. Walter looked distressed when pressed to tell about his own military career and simply commented; 'It's nothing like as interesting as the tale you have just heard.'

***

Emily's big problem remained, how to persuade Walter to treat their marriage as a partnership rather than a dictatorship. When he suggested that she should take full charge of decorating and furnishing their new home; she could not have been more pleased and they kissed and cuddled, just like in the old days. Her Jimmy had once more become the happy, relaxed man she married and perhaps her worries about him dominating her were over.

It fell to her to choose the colour of paint for the walls; she would have preferred wallpaper but the builder advised against this as the plaster needed time to dry. She chose a pale cream throughout, a complete contrast to the flat in Beckenham.

Furnishing the sitting room and dining room to her taste provided a real challenge. She qualified for Utility furniture as someone who had been bombed out but wanted something better. Walter provided the answer, explaining:

'When people die their furniture and valuable antiques are often sold by auction. I'll give you a list of promising auctions of large houses and a budget of how much to spend. Go and see if there's anything you like but don't get carried away with the bidding. Fix a maximum for each item you like and stick to it.'

She found auctions fascinating and soon acquired by this means a dining room table and chairs, a desk for Walter, a beautiful Queen Anne bureau for displaying ornaments and various other items which gave her much pleasure.

Meanwhile, her husband struggled to make something of the garden. He planted King Edward potatoes for food; a variety of rose bushes to add colour and fenced off a small enclosure to keep six hens. The hens were not a success; they did lay eggs but when he killed one of them for dinner, Emily could not face plucking the bird or handling its warm flesh. The ensuing row ended with mutual apologies and warm hugs.

***

Richard travelled back home to Keighley by train in the school holidays and went with his parents to visit Grandfather James, granny and Aunt Annie at weekends. He increasingly ventured out of Hebden Bridge on long walks to explore the country side with its fresh air and magnificent views. Occasionally his aunt, who liked hiking, would accompany him but as he got older he roamed far and wide by himself.

Emily did not approve of this, but Walter insisted: 'Our teenage son is old enough to look after himself. He must be allowed some independence and exercise. Surely you can see that?'

One Sunday, Richard set off up the steep hill to Heptonstall to see the ruined church damaged by Parliamentary cannon fire early in the civil war. Then, instead of his usual route to Hardcastle Crags, he headed in the opposite direction towards Black Shaw Head and up onto the moors from where he could see for miles.

He found a granite rock in the middle of nowhere on which to sit and eat his egg sandwiches. As he ate, he noticed a mist creeping up one of the valleys towards him but decided to finish his lunch then make his way downhill back to Hebden Bridge.

It came as a shock to realise that the innocuous mist had metamorphosed into thick fog. The view disappeared; he could only see a few yards. He thought: 'Better take a short-cut back to the road, but where is the road?' He knew where it should be and set off in that direction, treading carefully so as not to trip over any of the boulders and loose stones strewn all over the moor.

After half an hour, he could find still no trace of the road and decided to select a suitable rock to take a rest. The one just a little higher up the hill looked ideal: horror of horrors it proved to be the very rock where he ate his lunch. There could be no doubt about it, the skin from his orange lay accusingly at his feet.

Fog deadens sound; all around him silence, eerie silence – no wind, nothing moved, only the steady drip of moisture from a nearby tree. Then, he detected a faint rustle from the vicinity of a ruined low stone wall. 'Must have gone too far west,' he confided to a nervous rabbit which made a mad scramble to its burrow.

The light drizzle trickling down his neck did not improve his mood, but at least his boots were sound. He resolved to be positive, no future in hanging around; he would retrace his steps over the original route and tick off in his mind the landmarks as he recognised them. A sudden puff of wind; a gap in the cloud cover gave him hope. As he descended, the fog gradually lifted and he made it back to Hebden Bridge much later than planned to a worried Emily and an angry father.

**

Walter decided that before Richard took his 'O' level exam in French, the family should spend two weeks in France to find out for themselves how Parisians really spoke the language. Unfortunately, the Exchange Control Regulations only allowed fifty pounds per person to be taken out of Britain so they would have to live frugally.

The holiday began in Paris but dinner, even in the modest hotel where they were staying, proved to be too expensive after the first day. The French were rude about English food, claiming that the British with their rationing lived off boiled cabbage and potatoes.

Emily commented to her family: 'The French can't boast; they live off rabbit, wild bird pate and frogs legs. But undeniably, the standard of French cooking, even in modest establishments, far exceeds what we have in the United Kingdom and they do not suffer from our rationing and food shortages.'

On their first day, the family strolled down the Champs Elise to see the Arc de Triomphe; Richard a few paces in front of his parents who revelled in the romance of the city and held hands. To his acute embarrassment, a teenage French girl about his own age sidled up beside him and deliberately kept in step.

Walter considered the episode hugely amusing and told his son: 'You really should not consort with loose ladies in front of your mother. We did not bring you here to make an exhibition of yourself with sexy French girls.'

Paris had largely avoided the terrible destruction suffered by London and other British cities during the war, but the population had endured three years of German occupation. People hated collaborators and the carefree atmosphere of the 1930s no longer existed.

The second part of the holiday entailed a short trip on the Blue Train, a famous express connecting Paris with the French Riviera, from which they alighted at Amboise. This beautiful small town on the banks of the river Loire is famous for its chateau and its history.

There, they stayed at the Auberge du Mail and took day trips to nearby Clemenceau with its magnificent chateau and walked in the nearby forests, finding it much more relaxing than Paris. A forester, previously a member of the French Resistance, on learning that Walter had served in the British Army during the war, gave each of them a glass of delicious local wine.

Amboise proved too relaxed for Walter; he tried to cash his travellers' cheques at the local bank only to be confronted by the manager who demanded: 'Who is this Lloyds Bank? The name means nothing to me, it is not on my list of banks.' It took several telephone calls to London and Paris before the manager's head office confirmed that he could pay against a Lloyds Bank travellers' cheque.

***

One afternoon back home in Keighley, Emily received a telephone call from Mary, her long forgotten little sister: 'Please come to see mother. She's suffering from an incurable disease and badly wants to see you and your son before she dies. I've been asked to invite you all to lunch at father's house in Halifax next Saturday at half past twelve prompt.'

Emily initially wanted to decline but Walter persuaded her to accept the invitation: 'Richard should see his grandmother at least once even if we never go a second time.'

They arrived at the grandparents' home smartly dressed in their best Sunday clothes; Emily wearing her fashionable red dress and hat and Richard his school uniform. His father warned him: 'You had better be on your very best behaviour young man and don't say a word unless someone speaks to you. Is that understood?'

Emily's father and mother ushered them straight into the dining room and seated them at the round mahogany dinner table she knew so well. She felt too embarrassed to look her father in the eye much less speak to him and her mother did not say a word. Her younger sister, now married, no longer lived in the house and did not put in an appearance.

It fell to Walter to break the embarrassing silence by announcing: 'I expect you know that I am the new manager of Lloyds Bank Keighley and that this is my son, Richard, who is a pupil at Dulwich College in London.' They did know from their younger daughter and that attempt at conversation died the death.

The mother served the first course which, true to Yorkshire tradition, consisted of Yorkshire pudding smothered in treacle. Emily felt proud to see Richard struggle with this new experience, trying not to grimace and manfully finishing the serving.

The meal passed without hardly a word being spoken but, when it mercifully ended, Emily felt obliged to help her sick mother with the washing up. 'You stay there,' her father commanded. 'You're obviously much too grand to dirty your hands. It's enough that you've honoured us with your presence.'

They left immediately and Walter told his family: 'We've done our duty and there's no need to repeat the experience.' Emily's mother died a few months later and she did not attend the funeral, indeed she never spoke to her father again.

**

That summer, Walter made a last minute decision to take the family on holiday to the Norfolk Broads despite the fact that none of them had any experience with boats. Clearly, they could not handle a yacht but he managed to hire a converted life boat, no longer seaworthy but considered safe enough for the calm though tidal rivers of the Broads.

On the family's arrival at St Olaves Marina, the craft turned out to be large and unwieldy, big enough to sleep seven adults. Moreover, the powerful diesel engine proved difficult to start and the gear box stiff and unreliable. However, no other boats were available in the peak holiday season and Walter felt convinced that his experience with motor cycle engines would see him through.

Emily kept her doubts to herself; she needed a break as much as anyone and the sunshine and relaxed holiday atmosphere persuaded her to accept the adventure. Richard's enthusiasm and impatience to be on their way settled the matter and off they went down the river Waveney in the direction of Great Yarmouth and the sea, intending to head up the river Bure to the North Broads.

At least, they had the river very much to themselves and took it in turns to steer the boat and learn how to handle it. The power of the engine impressed all of them but they were in no hurry and cruised along peacefully until they came to the junction with the river Yare. There, the current and falling tide made it necessary for the engine to show its strength. Experienced boatmen would have timed their arrival to the turn of the tide but anyone was allowed to drive a boat without any training!

The first week of the holiday went well; the north broads are truly serene and peaceful when the sun shines. Horning in particular is a beautiful village, the back gardens of its houses and thatched cottages extend to the waters' edge and often incorporate a mooring. However, in the peak of the season it is thronged with boats and sightseers and difficult to find a place to land anywhere along the Staithe.

Walter had promised Emily that he would buy lunch at the old Swan Inn but they could not find a suitable spot to moor their boat. He did not react well when a large yacht insisted on exercising its right of way, cutting his engine speed and wrenching the gear into neutral but failing to engage reverse. A collision became inevitable, but fortunately Richard did find reverse and avoided serious damage to either vessel.

The real drama occurred on the final night of the holiday when torrential rain and thunder and lightning lashed the Broads. Before the storm, Emily had selected a secluded spot where they tied the boat to a mooring post on the river bank and sat down at a table in the galley to enjoy their last dinner on board, intending to stay the night and enjoy the almost total silence around them.

The tide came up and the deluge flooded the river, causing the water level to rise and lift the boat off its mooring. It came as a shock to realise that they were drifting downstream towards the sea in pitch darkness, the moon obscured by thunder clouds.

Walter struggled to start the engine, leaving Emily and Richard to try and discover where they were when lightning lit up the landscape. When the boat eventually got under way, they steered into the fast flowing main channel and headed upstream away from the sea, the powerful engine barely succeeding in keeping the boat on its course.

As dawn broke, the storm subsided, the tide turned and peace returned. Emily vowed never to go to the Broads again and to keep away from small boats.

***

Chapter 19

Chislehurst

December 1957

Walter made a success of Keighley Branch and gained promotion to Lloyds Bank's Head Office where he eventually became Chief Inspector. This made it necessary for the family to move back to London and they decided to live in Chislehurst. Emily had fond memories of the area from pre-war days despite the trauma of being bombed, but missed her friends and the home in Keighley which she had spent so much care lovingly creating.

Walter promised: 'I'll buy an even better house for us in Chislehurst,' and this he did, the property's only real defect being its position close to the mainline railway, the same line as their original house in Petts Wood. Emily would have preferred to live further away from the railway but her reservations were ignored. She began to worry that Walter's dictatorial tendencies were reasserting themselves again now that he had the stress of commuting to London and working in Head Office.

The new house, like their home in Keighley, contained three bedrooms but these in Chislehurst were larger and the through lounge boasted windows on three sides making it light and airy. Equally important to Emily, the substantial garden had been landscaped and attractively planted with mature trees and flower beds. It seemed to be a happy house and she began planning how to turn the property into the home of her dreams. She loved Walter and if he still loved her, he must allow her to redecorate their new home to her own taste.

She set about ordering wallpaper; red Regency stripes for the hall, stairs and landing, a large floral pattern of roses for the lounge and pale cream for the two main bedrooms. After much thought, she selected expensive plum coloured Wilton carpets for downstairs, with cheaper tufted cream carpets in the bedrooms.

Curtains were more of a problem as she wanted to use those they had brought from Yorkshire where possible. Similarly, their own furniture fitted well into the new house, with the luxury addition of a mahogany cocktail cabinet purchased from Harrods to give the lounge an impression of opulence.

***

Emily felt proud of her son's achievements; he had graduated from University College London and now worked as an articled clerk (trainee) with a firm of solicitors in the City of London. Although 21, he still lived at home and she worried if he came home late.

On the night of the Lewisham train crash in December 1957, she and Walter learned of the crash on the news and became increasingly alarmed when Richard failed to come home or telephone to say that he would be staying in town.

In dense fog, the steam locomotive express to Ramsgate had crashed into the back of a packed commuter train stopped at a red signal. The accident dislodged the pier of a bridge carrying a third train over the main line causing it to collapse and completely blocking all four tracks running under the bridge and the two tracks over it. This disaster killed ninety people and injured countless others.

Another crowded commuter train carrying Richard followed immediately behind the express and became stuck between stations. Eventually, the stunned railway authorities allowed it to creep into New Cross, a minor station quite unable to cope with the thousand or so disgruntled passengers who alighted. There, they learned that their train would be returning to the London terminal and no trains would be available to take them home that evening.

Richard and a handful of others decided to walk to Lewisham and see if trains bound for London were being turned round there but the thickness of the fog made this difficult. Fire engines and ambulances, bells ringing and sirens blaring, converged on them from all sides followed by a large vehicle proclaiming itself to be the Control Centre.

Little more than a mile down the road, they found their way blocked by police who told them of the train crash and directed them down a side road to Lewisham High Street. The street lights enabled Richard to recognise the A20 main road; the route his father always took when driving into London.

Chislehurst lay ten miles away, dare he attempt to walk there in the fog? A slightly older man, a complete stranger, announced that he lived in Sidcup, a suburb near Chislehurst, and proposed to walk down the A20 if anyone would join him. So off the two of them set, best foot forward and made good progress under the street lights.

Once out of Lewisham, the street lamps petered out and after a while, they ran into a patch of fog so thick that they could hardly see their feet. The absence of any traffic on the normally busy road struck them; they were alone and to make matters worse had no torch to help them cling to the verge.

The eerie sound of bells and sirens approaching forced them off the tarmac. A sad procession of three fire-engines, sent from a coastal town to help their London colleagues, crept into view, lights blazing, but travelling at no more than ten miles an hour.

'If those poor devils can do it, so can we,' Richard told his wilting companion who now regretted the whole idea of hiking in the fog. They struggled on for miles until at last they reached the traffic lights and cross road from Chislehurst to Sidcup. 'Now I know exactly where we are,' Richard announced brightly. 'You cross the road and go down there to Sidcup; whilst I turn right into Chislehurst.'

'Please don't leave me,' the older man pleaded. 'I can't go much further. My feet hurt.' Richard pointed at the traffic light on the far side of the road. 'Once you reach that light, fifty yards further on Sidcup officially starts. Keep straight on and you'll be in the High Street; you really have made it!' They parted and never saw one another again.

Richard's own problems were far from over, he still had three miles to go down an unlit road by himself with the fog growing ever denser as he went downhill. No one else had ventured out in such conditions and the silence and trees created a macabre effect. The dark never frightened him, but the fog reminded him of his own experience on the Yorkshire moors and added a new dimension of horror; he gritted his teeth and pressed on following the signs to the station.

Once there, he walked down a road he knew well which ran parallel with the railway, until finally his own front gate emerged from the gloom. The house lay hidden by the fog but he knew that gate and marched confidently up to the front door. As he fumbled for the correct key, he became aware of another presence dressed in black in the garden. In a panic, he put the wrong key in the lock and it failed to open.

A hand on his shoulder and a distinctly hostile voice: 'What do you think you are doing young man?'

He turned to see a policeman shining a torch in his face. 'I live here,' he gasped. 'I'll ring the bell and they'll identify me.'

The hand pulled him away. 'No we won't. We don't want to disturb the nice people who live here. Been out for a stroll in the fog have we but forgot your torch?'

Richard found the sarcasm annoying but the menacing tone quite alarming. 'I really do live here. I can prove it.' But how could he prove it?

'Got a key to the garage have you? Well then tell me the make of car which we'll find inside and the registration number.'

He did, to the astonishment of the policeman when they opened the garage door. The officer apologised and shone his torch on the front door to help the former suspect find the right key and let himself into the house. Emily hugged her son for a whole three minutes, too relieved to see him alive to scold him, and made him tell her all about his adventure.

***

When Richard qualified as a solicitor in 1959, there were very few lady solicitors. The profession survived by using experienced managing clerks to deal with routine matters and only when these eventually retired were women recruited to replace them. Computers and word processors did not exist; all letters and documents needed to be dictated to shorthand typists and their wages were low enough for every fee earner to have his own secretary.

Richard would tell Emily about some of the amazing people he came into contact with and she enjoyed reliving the experience with him.

'Today on my travels, I found myself sharing a train compartment with a South African Boer from Durban who insisted on chatting for virtually the whole journey. The man expressed astonishment at the way the British press is allowed to report on terrorist activities saying that at home they suffer many bomb attacks but keep them secret so as not to alarm the population.

'The Boer strongly supported Apartheid; he believed that the black population are just as keen on keeping the races separate as the white. When I protested at such heresy, he told me about his experience when visiting Zululand on business he had with one of the chiefs.

'Driving north, he reached a road block where the South African police warned him that if he went any further, they would not be able to protect him. He produced his invitation from the Zulu Chief and proceeded on his way.

'After contracts were signed, the Chief's mother asked to meet the Boer. He stretched out his hand to greet her but the mother shrank away and fled from the room. The Chief told him: "You must excuse her. She has never seen a white man before and could not bring herself to touch you."

***

Within days of Richard qualifying as a solicitor, the senior partner in his firm despatched him to make a liquor licensing application to a metropolitan magistrate. To his alarm, the clerk informed him that his application would be heard first. He had barely uttered the words: 'I appear on behalf of …' when the magistrate interrupted: 'Yes, yes, I have read the papers, application granted.'

Richard resumed his seat with a view to hearing some of the morning's cases but a policeman rushed over and instructed him: 'Please gather your papers together and come with me. He did you a favour by taking you first. It's Monday morning. If you stay all the prostitutes and drunks arrested on Saturday night will apply to have you as their dock brief and you'll be stuck here all day.'

He made a firm decision not to become involved in criminal law when a few weeks later he sat behind counsel representing three men who pleaded guilty to the charges against them. The magistrate asked the police prosecutor: 'Anything known?' and received a negative response. The accused were dismissed with a caution but outside the court one of them turned to Richard and confessed: 'Nothing known. That must have cost a bob or two; I've done time in Dartmoor.'

***

One morning, Richard received a call from the reception desk in his office: 'There's a man without an appointment who wants to see you. He won't give me his name but looks very respectable.' Was there just the hint of a giggle in the receptionist's voice?

Full of curiosity, he went to reception to discover a strikingly fit young man in his late twenties wearing a smart pin stripe suit. 'Forgive me if I do not give you a name; you have been recommended to me as reliable by one of your firm's clients. I don't need legal advice, but if you agree to make a telephone call for me, I'll pay you one hundred pounds in cash now.'

The pleading look in the speaker's eyes contrasted with his self-confident manner. Intrigued and suspecting a practical joke, Richard enquired: 'Who should I call and what should I say'?

'Please make an appointment for me to see you a week on Friday. If I keep it, I will explain then. If I don't, simply ring this number and tell them that the pilot is missing. There won't be anything they can do but it will be some comfort for me to know that my friends are aware that I did not make it back.' He handed over a piece of paper with a telephone number written on it.

Richard insisted: 'You must give me a little more information in case a secretary answers the phone and refuses to take the message seriously.' The young man nodded and named a country in Africa; they shook hands and the visitor paid the money and left.

A week later, Richard saw the appointment burning a hole in his diary page. People do not pay money just to make someone sound stupid on the telephone and the expression in the young man's eyes made him believe that he should take the matter seriously.

On Wednesday morning, the front pages of most British papers carried headlines proclaiming that the President of the country concerned had been assassinated in an armed uprising against its Government. Richard forced himself to remain calm and do nothing until the appointed time. He did, however, share his concerns with Emily in case something untoward happened to him. She remonstrated with him for indulging in such matters.

He need not have been alarmed; the very next day after the coup, the pilot reappeared in his office. 'Don't worry; I didn't shoot anyone. My job is to fly the plane, find and land in the designated clearing in the jungle, turn her round, keep the engine running and above all avoid looking at the faces of the men who take the stuff out of the back. You'll never see me again.'

A few years later Richard asked a friend whether the fresh scar on his lower lip had been caused by a car accident. The reply astonished him: 'Whilst on holiday on the south coast, I took a sightseeing trip in a light aircraft, just me and the pilot. Another similar plane took a tight turn but not tight enough and crashed into our tail. We watched its wing snap off and they spiralled down to crash on a pebbly beach where the plane exploded; there could have been no survivors.

'My pilot stayed icily calm and enquired: "Do you want me to land the plane on the beach or ditch it in the sea? The damage to our tail makes it impossible for us to make it back to the airfield; we are going down whatever I do."

'I tried to tell him that I could not swim, but bit my lip so hard that no words came out. I bit right through and the scar you see is where the hospital stitched the wound together. The pilot could not understand why I did not reply. He told me: "Don't worry, no one is shooting at us." We landed in the sea and the plane started to sink. He yelled at me: "Get out! With a hole in the tail, we only have two or three minutes at the most before she sinks."

'I stayed sitting in my seat, petrified and unable to move. He showed no sign of fear, pulled me out and told me to swim to the shore. I thrashed about and went under but he swam back; dragged me to safety and resuscitated me.'

Richard wondered if it was the same pilot as the one who had refused to give his name.

***

Chapter 20

A Second Honeymoon

September 1970

One afternoon, whilst lounging in a deck chair in her garden waiting in the sunshine for Walter to come home from the bank, Emily reflected on the targets that she had originally set herself all those years ago before the war. She told herself: 'I've married my Jimmy who does treat me as an equal when he's not under stress and I have my precious Richard, a pity we never had more children. I must make a special effort to get really close to my husband again.'

That evening as they climbed into bed together, Walter announced: 'One of my customers told me today about a fantastic camping holiday he and his wife enjoyed in the south of France. Apparently, it's quite cheap if you go out of season in September when the children are back at school.'

As Emily rolled over onto her back, she thought: 'Whoopee!' But she simply said: 'If that's what you want dearest; are you going to give me a cuddle?'

He kissed her on the cheek and murmured in her ear: 'Dear Betty, thank you for being so understanding with me all these past years. We could find somewhere really nice in France or even in Spain to take a long holiday. I suggest we take a second honeymoon.' Before she could reply, they slid into an embrace every bit as passionate as any she could remember.

The following morning over breakfast, Emily enquired: 'Jimmy, did you really mean what you said last night? Can I begin to make plans about where we go in Europe? Or would you simply prefer to have a fortnight on one of the Greek Islands? I'll make enquiries from some of our friends about where they recommend for a holiday.'

'You decide,' he replied. 'I have to go to work.'

She smiled happily; touring Spain would be best. She liked France, perhaps not Paris – she remembered the teenage street girl marching in step with Richard, but several of her friends swore by Cordoba and the south of Spain which she had never seen.

As she watched him hurry down the drive, the full significance of his remark struck her. He really had left the decision to her; for the first time in their relationship, she had been encouraged to take the lead in deciding where they should spend their holiday. She hummed a happy little tune to herself *singing in the rain, I'm singing in the rain.*

They spent the next few days packing all they would need and making arrangements for their trip. 'We won't book any hotels, then we're free to go where we want and can stay for as long or short a time as we like. I suggest we head for the south of Spain; I'd like to be somewhere warm. Is that alright with you?' Emily enquired with a catch in her voice.

He nodded: 'Whatever you say is fine by me.'

***

Up as dawn broke on what promised to be a glorious late September day, they caught an early morning ferry to Calais and after a long drive down French motorways arrived at their first planned destination, Chateauroux, around dinner time.

'I've chosen this after consulting the Michelin Guide,' Emily confided. 'The *Jeux 2 Gouts* serves one of the best meals in France and I want to start our second honeymoon with something truly memorable.'

They entered the restaurant to be greeted by a surprised receptionist: 'You haven't booked. We only have six tables and patrons book at least three months in advance.' Then she smiled: 'but we've just had a cancellation. You are extremely fortunate; just have a seat there and I'll bring you the menu and an appetiser of pink champagne. The chef will come and advise you shortly.'

The chef duly arrived: 'Tell me whether you want a main course of meat, fish or fowl. I'll then recommend the best I have and the vegetables to go with it. Of course, you can have anything else on the menu if you prefer.'

They followed his advice, ate a truly memorable, delicious meal and the receptionist booked them in at a nearby hotel. She told them: 'There is something special you ought to see in the morning, it's a renaissance style castle set in thirty six hectares of parklands in the midst of a small village. In the 15th century, a comrade in arms of King Louis XI built the keep and later four wings featuring Italian style galleries were added. One wing was destroyed during the French Revolution; another has been transformed into a comfortable dwelling which is now for sale.'

Next day, curiosity caused them to drive out to the chateau which proved to be even larger than they had expected with two huge reception rooms designed to accommodate hunting parties. Both contained enormous fireplaces and stone floors. But everywhere, the place smelt of decay and repairs to make it habitable would cost a fortune; even the river had been choked by fallen trees and the stables, cottages and other outbuildings had no rooves.

'This is definitely not for us,' Walter remarked, 'but let's have a cup of coffee in the village and look round the old church.'

They went through the postern gate into the churchyard and both gasped and looked at one another in horror. The church gargoyles, designed to frighten away devils, were revolting and the village street looked dark and shoddy. 'Let's forget about coffee and get away from this miserable place,' Emily pleaded.

'I'm not surprised the villagers revolted. Do you think they guillotined the owners of the chateau?'

***

The next stage of their journey took them to Biarritz on the Atlantic coast of France close to the boarder with Spain, once a favourite holiday spot for British nobility. They could not compete with the affluent holiday-makers in designer gear or afford to stay at the Hotel le Regina but instead opted for a cheap modern hotel to the west of the resort.

On their second day, Emily announced: 'I don't like it here, the grand houses on the cliff top overlooking the beach are all in ruins. Look the back walls of several buildings have collapsed onto the sand.'

***

Cordoba, chosen by Emily after studying numerous holiday brochures, became their next destination. The town, founded by the Romans on the banks of the Guadalquivir River, used to be the capital of the Moorish kingdom of El-Andalus. The Moors built the Great Mosque, one of the largest in all Islam. When the Christians reconquered the city, they left the Mosque standing, building their own cathedral in the midst of its rows of arches and marble pillars, creating an extraordinary church-mosque.

Walter and Emily booked into a comfortable hotel, Hotel Lola, directly opposite to the Mosque and after dinner retired to bed. 'There are so many things to see and do here,' Emily murmured in her husband's ear. 'I'm so happy we came; are you?' In reply, he kissed her on the lips and they made love for the first time in Spain.

Next morning, they explored the Mosque and marvelled at its size and the grandeur of its arches and alcoves. The sound of organ music attracted their attention and they discovered a catholic service in progress, a hymn being sung by a solitary elderly nun whilst the congregation listened in silence.

'How strange,' Emily commented. 'It doesn't seem right to hold such a service in the middle of this magnificent mosque or is it still a mosque? It gives me the creeps to hear a nun singing a Christian hymn here - none of the congregation are joining in; let's go.'

They walked along the historic streets taking in the scent of orange blossom, the strains of a Spanish guitar and several tempting tapas bars, before selecting the *Garum* to sample its gazpacho and squid croquettes. After their snack, they explored the *Palacio de Viana*, a Renaissance palace set around twelve magnificent patios with gardens and fountains to soothe away the stress of life.

Emily squeezed Walter's hand: 'Have you ever seen anything so beautiful as that artificial lake, the clear blue water and the reflection of the turrets and palm trees in the background?'

In the evening, they celebrated a successful first day in Cordoba by dining outside on the patio of the *Puerta Sevilla* restaurant. There they sampled anchovies on toast and tomato with smoked sardine before dining on shellfish soup and Iberian pork, then finishing off with fondant and a glass of sherry. The town hums until late into the night so they strolled hand in hand along the river to the beguiling Roman Bridge before retiring exhausted to bed.

The following day they explored the *Alcazar* which had been alternately a fortress and a palace with yet more Roman mosaics and Moorish courtyards; it boasted a particularly fine set of fountains and ponds. Emily suggested: 'Let's book to see the flamenco dancers one evening and also the prancing horses of Andalusia at the Royal Stables.'

As time went by and the sun got hotter, Emily remarked: 'I love this place but now we've seen it all. It's getting time to move on to somewhere cooler, but before we leave Spain I'd like to go to Granada and perhaps explore the *Alhambra*.' Walter grinned as he nodded his approval.

***

The size and magnificence of the *Alhambra* far exceeded Emily's expectations. 'Oh look,' she exclaimed pointing at a brochure, 'it's described as "a pearl set in emeralds filled with the sound of running water. Column arcades, fountains with running water and reflecting pools add to the aesthetic beauty; the exterior being left plain and austere. All the rooms open on to a central court following the consistent theme of paradise on earth". This is something we really must explore.'

They followed the crowd into the heart of the complex to discover that it contained six palaces in all with numerous bath houses set in thirty five acres. The Royal suite with its brightly coloured panels and decorated ceilings and particularly the grand reception room in the Hall of the Ambassadors amazed Emily as did the Court of Lions with its spectacular fountain.

After wandering around hand in hand for four hours in the heat of the day, Emily gasped: 'I'm thirsty and the sun is too strong. Shall we call it a day and return to our hotel in Granada? There's too much to absorb here in one day but I vote we leave Spain and take a look at the French Riviera.'

As they crossed the French border, Walter commented: 'Thank goodness it's a little cooler here. I wouldn't want to stay in Spain and I suggest we give Italy a miss as well. Let's keep away from the traffic on the coast road and take the motorways to spend the night in Grasse where they make perfume; then in the morning make for Monte Carlo and work our way back slowly along the Riviera to Cannes.'

Emily gave his arm a squeeze and beamed: 'Ooh! There is a perfume I'd like to try; it's called *Le Train Bleu*.'

Next day they explored Monte Carlo and found it smaller than they had expected and their lunch much more expensive. 'This place is beautiful but ruinous,' Walter exclaimed. So off they headed to Cap d' Antibes where Emily to her disgust discovered nude bathers lying on the rocks; then Nice where she saw a prostitute parading in a side street just off the *Promenade des Anglais*.

Cannes, however, both of them enjoyed and they strolled hand in hand along La Croisette, the splendid promenade curving around the bay with a sparkling acreage of shiny sea out front and exotic palm trees in the middle of the road. Here, they mingled happily with over-tanned ladies dressed in furs and admired the palatial hotels lined up on the other side of the road – the Majestic Hotel and beyond it the Carlton and the Hotel Martinez.

On cooler days they continued their promenade round the bay all the way to the casino at the Pointe de la Croisette headland or in the opposite direction up Suquet hill which rises up from the old port in a labyrinth of narrow streets and steep stairways. On another day, they took the ferry to the comparative solitude of Ste Margarite, one of the Iles des Lerins a few minutes boat ride off shore. Later, they took a coach trip up the hill behind the city to the observatory with its magnificent views over the Riviera and its azure sea.

One evening over an exotic dinner outside a back street restaurant, Walter suggested: 'We've seen Cannes now but the place is expensive and it's nearly time to return home. My vote is that we take a look at St Tropez then explore Cavalaire-sur-mer with its sandy beach where we can stop exploring and relax'.

Emily smiled: 'Whatever **you** want, Jimmy. I do love you, I really do; this trip has been a superb way of celebrating our second honeymoon.' He smiled and gave her a peck on the cheek.

***

St Tropez, with artists painting and selling pictures around its sizeable harbour full of large expensive yachts, intrigued them. Emily commented: 'The brightly painted houses and castle on the hill are a really attractive setting. It could be a poor man's Monte Carlo except that the boats tied to the quay, the designer clothes in the shops and the prices in the restaurants are really expensive. Yet the place is crowded with coach loads of day trippers like us who come to stare but buy little more than a cup of coffee.'

Then she discovered the huge open air market and spent an hour or two inspecting the stalls in a search for bargains. One or two of the paintings on display very nearly tempted her but she reluctantly realised that they would look out of place back home in England.

After half a day in St Tropez, they moved on to find a hotel in Cavalaire-sur-Mer with its palm trees, pines and the sea. The holiday-time gaiety of the resort and its surroundings were breath-taking, a long stretch of sand punctuated by beach restaurants and sprinkled with semi-nude bathers looked hot but idyllic. The rugged Cap Lardier headland and in the opposite direction the Îles d'Or shimmering offshore in the distance provided a superb setting.

They soon realised that the yacht harbour, with its bars and restaurants catering for all prices, provided the focal point for visitors. The constant movement of boats of all shapes and sizes in and out of their berths fascinated both of them.

Sitting in the late afternoon sunshine on the terrace of the Blue Anchor, sipping Pina colada and watching a motor cruiser not twenty yards away expertly backing into its mooring, Emily mused: 'Cavalaire is close to but so different from St Tropez; no air of exclusivity here, normal people like me are made to feel welcome at the bars and restaurants. People don't dress up here.'

She waved to Walter coming out of a restaurant, which specialised in fish and oysters caught by the local fishermen early that very morning, where he had gone to book a table for dinner that evening.

As he strolled towards her down the quay, she thought: 'I'm so lucky to be here in the sunshine; it's far beyond the dreams I had all those years ago when I eloped. That was the best decision I ever made; Walter, bless him, does treat me as an equal now. We followed our dreams and here we are despite the war and all the horrendously difficult times which we faced along the way! We have at last finally settled down to enjoy married life together, in peace.'

***

Epilogue

Britain Pre and Post World War 2

This fact based novel portrays the life of a loving family in order to give the reader an idea of what it was like living in Britain during the middle of the twentieth century.

Britain had been gravely damaged by the First World War and people were strongly opposed to reliving the suffering yet again, a horror still fresh in their memory after a mere twenty years. That War cost around ten million lives, eight hundred thousand of them British, leaving many more crippled but victory did not bring happiness. Britain remained far from the land fit for heroes promised to the soldiers and this caused considerable disquiet.

The incompetent generals of the so called Great War were never brought to account; while shell shocked troops had been shot as cowards. A sense of injustice, of inability to achieve one's full potential, produced not merely socialists, but communists and fascists in our midst.

A real danger existed in the 1920s that the Russian revolution might spread to Britain. Troops became restive at the delay in demobilising them, fearing that the Government might send them to Russia to fight the Bolsheviks. Then again, many soldiers and sailors became unemployed and did not even have homes for their families.

The war cost an estimated forty billion pounds sterling, a currency then linked to the gold standard and worth far more than the pound today. This left the country burdened with a national debt which the Government declined to increase by launching much needed housing and other projects financed at the taxpayers' expense. Preserving the exchange rate of the currency and avoiding inflation received absolute priority, regardless of the suffering this caused; a mistake mirrored in the austerity imposed after the recent recession.

The unemployment and poverty led to riots and a series of major damaging strikes by railway workers, miners, in the shipyards and in many other industries culminating in the General strike of 1926, but no revolution except in Ireland.

The adversity caused by the General strike produced a great patriotic response which weakened the unions and the Labour party. The outlook briefly improved for a time, until any hope of prosperity was dashed by the Stock Market crash in the United States which rumbled round the world. This caused unemployment and poverty to continue in Britain through the 1930s, until the country began belatedly to rearm in 1938.

The economic problems of the 1920s stemmed from the massive war debts incurred during the First World War which imposed an intolerable strain on the world's economies. The crippling repayments to the United States gave the appearance of increasing prosperity in that country, leading to an orgy of optimism and speculation based on cheap credit. Economists, bankers and the stock market persuaded themselves that economic cycles were a thing of the past, rather as they did before the crash in this century.

And why did the optimism and speculation suddenly end in the Great Crash on 21st October 1929? Four years earlier in 1925, Britain had restored its currency to the gold standard at the pre-war rate, a rate which at that time seriously overvalued the pound. This damaged exports thereby increasing already high unemployment and industrial unrest. Imperial pride refused to accept that its economy had been weakened by the war.

Gold began to flow to New York in a steady and increasing stream; this needed to be reversed and it was. On 26th September 1929, the Bank of England dramatically raised its Base Rate by one per cent to 6.5%, a move followed by a number of other countries. This forced the United States to increase its own interest rates with devastating consequences for speculators and members of the public who had overextended themselves by relying on cheap loans.

Britain's rigid class structure somehow survived the First World War. This reluctance to educate and promote able working class men and women and corrupting nepotism weakened the country. Famous public schools continued to produce leaders of the nation,

The wealthy and aristocracy lived in luxury, though not to the same extent as they did before the First World War. They, like everyone else, lost relatives and friends killed and wounded; they too suffered from a paucity of eligible bachelors. Servants were harder to come-by and more expensive; the returning heroes had seen something of the world and were no longer prepared to spend their lives in service. And then came the crash which ruined many, though not the landed gentry.

Three million unemployed and their families were at the opposite end of the scale. Unemployment benefit was but a dream for the future; starvation a real threat. There were hunger marches to draw their plight to the attention of the nation.

War work had demonstrated that women were at least as capable as men to do less physical jobs. They saw no reason not to continue in those jobs when the war ended. Because they accepted low wages and had taken positions previously held by men, this exacerbated male unemployment. The suffragettes won votes for women but only gradually after considerable struggle and sacrifice.

Even so, in 1939 the country rose up and once again fought for freedom with a steadfastness and courage which future generations can only applaud. Moreover, Britain still had the unswerving support of a powerful Empire.

***

The start of the Second World War could hardly have been better timed for Britain. Any earlier and it would not have had enough Spitfires to beat off the German air offensive in the Blitz. Any later and Hitler would have brought into mass production the secret weapons and rockets which his scientists did succeed in developing towards the end of the conflict.

The Allies came close to disaster on a number of occasions, but fortunately Hitler insisted on imposing his own strategy on the German High Command and made serious errors of judgment against their advice. In particular, he switched targets in the Blitz away from airfields and munitions factories to bombing London and other cities. Even more calamitous for Germany, he attacked Russia - then his ally - opening up a second front rather than concentrating on attacking Britain.

Churchill also would have made some errors such as pressing on with the allied advance into the heavily defended mountainous terrain of Northern Italy, but each time either the War Cabinet or his Allies overruled him. His true greatness was not as a strategist, but as a leader who held together a defeated army after Dunkirk, inspired his people and led them to victory. He also held the Allies together during times of crisis, no easy task given that America, Russia and Britain had very different objectives once Hitler surrendered.

***

In the Second World War, women as well as men perished in the Blitz, and a number of girls left the country to marry Americans and Canadians. The disparity in the number of eligible men and women was far less than in 1918. A far higher proportion of couples married, as opposed to simply living together; divorce and bankruptcy carried a stigma as did homosexuality.

Serious concerns arose about how their families would receive troops returning home from the war? Returning troops were entitled by law to have their old jobs reinstated, assuming their employers still existed, but many found it difficult to adjust to civilian life after years away fighting a brutal enemy.

Soldiers trained to kill needed to exercise great restraint if embroiled in a pub brawl. Too often, they found that men who used to be their junior but had avoided military service, were now in senior positions. However, enlightened employers ensured that returning troops received rapid promotion once they became accustomed to civilian life.

With three million houses and other buildings destroyed in the Second World War, half of them in London, emergency steps were required to clear the bombsites and provide prefabricated bungalows for people to live in and resume their lives. This time, unlike after the First World War, work did exist for the returning troops. Only one in four houses were owner occupied; people could not afford to buy even with the help of a mortgage.

One noticeable effect of the war was the improvement in the position of women. So many men joined the armed forces that women took their chance to show what they could do. In 1946, one and a half million women were employed as secretaries who sat and took dictation in shorthand or as copy typists. The number of secretaries required today is far fewer due to the advent of computers.

Indeed, the process of emancipation accelerated as time passed and women became solicitors, barristers and judges, something virtually unheard of in the 1930s. In 1947, twenty two per cent of married women and most single adult women were in paid work. They now began to demand equal pay, though to this day they commonly receive less for much the same work.

How else did life differ from that we know today? London and other cities suffered from dense smog, a revolting mixture of smoke and fog, greatly reduced as a result of the Clean Air Act passed in 1993.

The war ended, but rationing and shortages continued into the 1950s. People worried about finding somewhere to live. Moreover, two years national service in the armed forces remained compulsory for men, one of the reasons why life remained so disciplined.

The concept of human rights did not exist, murderers hanged; delinquents could be beaten. Schoolchildren in particular were in real danger of being caned. Today, even convicted criminals and those who spurn their duties to society are accorded human rights!

Britain's rigid pre-war class structure, much derided by visiting American troops, never really recovered from the Second World War. The public schools still produced many of the leaders of the nation but several, like the Gilkes' experiment at Dulwich College, accepted able pupils from wider backgrounds.

The wealthy and the aristocracy continued to live in relative luxury, but a Socialist Government with a majority of 146 seats imposed swinging taxes and death duties that drastically affected their standard of living.

The British Commonwealth made great sacrifices for Britain in her hour of need; now they demanded and in most cases received independence. The loss of India in particular meant that Britain could never again match the power of the United States, though it took our leaders a long time to recognize that harsh reality. Once again our armed forces have dwindled to a fraction the size of those of many other nations.

Britain had spent her riches and found herself hugely in debt, particularly to the United States; the burden resulted in high taxes and greatly impoverished the nation. In 2007, Britain finally repaid to the United States the war debts arising from the Second World War.

Again, we see speculation based on cheap credit. Will the Authorities be more successful in managing the markets and peoples' lives this time? They seem inclined to seek solutions by holding interest rates low, but this time they printed money rather than making the mistake of returning to a modern equivalent of the gold standard. And the future? Ah, that is a secret closely attended by a bodyguard of lies which some call forecasts.

***

About the Author

James Lingard - educated at Dulwich College and University College London - became a leading City of London solicitor who specialized in banking law and insolvency.

A former Council Member of the Association of Business Recovery Professionals and of the European Association of Insolvency Practitioners, he became a Judicial Chairman of the Insolvency Practitioners Tribunal.

He was the founding President of the Insolvency Lawyers Association and also became Chairman of the Joint Insolvency Examination Board and of the Banking Law and the Insolvency Law Sub Committees of the City of London Law Society.

He is the original author of Lingard's Bank Security Documents (LexisNexis Butterworths) now in its 7th edition, a number of other legal books and of Britain At War 1939 to 1945 (Author House).

Lightning Source UK Ltd.
Milton Keynes UK
UKHW040625230120
357484UK00002B/424